D0540003

Please return/renew this item by the
last date shown to avoid a charge.
Books may also be renewed by phone
and Internet. May not be renewed if
required by another reader.

www.libraries.barnet.gov.uk

BARNET
LONDON BOROUGH

William Collins' dream of knowledge for all began with the publication of his first book in 1819.

A self-educated mill worker, he not only enriched millions of lives, but also founded a flourishing publishing house. Today, staying true to this spirit, Collins books are packed with inspiration, innovation and practical expertise. They place you at the centre of a world of possibility and give you exactly what you need to explore it.

Collins. Freedom to teach.
Published by Collins
An imprint of HarperCollins*Publishers*
The News Building
1 London Bridge Street
London
SE1 9GF

Browse the complete Collins catalogue at
www.collins.co.uk

The Alexander Text of the *Complete Works of William Shakespeare* was first published in 1951.
© HarperCollinsPublishers Limited 2019

10 9 8 7 6 5 4 3 2 1

ISBN 978-0-00-836360-4

British Library Cataloguing-in-Publication Data
A catalogue record for this publication is available from the British Library.

Text edited by Professor Peter Alexander
General Editor: R.B. Kennedy
Author of the introduction and theme and character index: Noel Cassidy
Author of the textual notes: Mike Gould
Cover designers: The Big Mountain
Typesetter: WhiteFox
Printed and bound by: CPI Group (UK) Ltd, Croydon, CR0 4YY

The publishers gratefully acknowledge the permission granted to reproduce the copyright material in this book. Every effort has been made to trace copyright holders and to obtain their permission for the use of copyright material. The publishers will gladly receive any information enabling them to rectify any error or omission at the first opportunity.

Contents

Introduction

Thunder and lightning. Fog. Three weird figures chant and question each other in a way that is difficult to understand. Macbeth's name is mentioned. From the first moments of the play, Shakespeare creates an atmosphere of threat and unease. The thunder and lightning suggest disorder in the elements, the fog makes everything indistinct, and as we know from Banquo's later descriptions, the three witches are strange – they are 'wild in their attire' and 'look not like th' inhabitants o' th' earth' (Act 1, Scene 3, lines 40–41). They mention warfare, which might also be heard through the thunder, and play with the meaning of words by equating 'foul' and 'fair' (Act 1, Scene 1, line 12). What can these mysterious figures want with Macbeth, the eponymous hero of the play?

By starting *Macbeth* with three witches, without any explanations, Shakespeare achieves a sudden, disorientating effect, plunging the audience into an uncanny but fascinating world. The audience's initial bewilderment at the ambiguous crones prefigures that of Macbeth and Banquo. As Shakespeare develops the language and action of the play, the importance of the supernatural, of what it means to be human, of overturning the logical opposition of 'fair' and 'foul', becomes more focused.

Shakespeare often used disorder in the natural world to mirror disorder in the human one. In the first scene of *Macbeth*, the disorder might refer to the battle, but the audience soon learns that the end of that battle does not bring peace and ease. The witches' invocation that 'Fair is foul, and foul is fair' (Act 1, Scene 1, line 12) provides a crucial bedrock for the play; Macbeth himself echoes the idea later (Act 1, Scene 3, line 38), and it runs through the rest of the drama – appearances are so deceptive that the characters, and sometimes the audience, are unsure who they can trust.

Themes in context
Witchcraft

In Elizabethan and Jacobean England many people believed in witchcraft and would have been intrigued by the sight of the three 'secret, black, and midnight hags' (Act 4, Scene 1, line 46). In a devoutly Christian society, witches and the dark arts were associated with the devil and seen to challenge God. Belief in them went to the very top of society: King James[1] believed that witches conspired against him and had published a study of the subject, called *Daemonologie*, in 1597. Shakespeare's focus on witches in *Macbeth* may have been one way in which he ensured his play reflected the spirit of the times; he may also have been flattering the king – after all, his theatre company received royal patronage and was known as The King's Men.

The Elizabethan and Jacobean periods were a time of superstition, when incidents of bad luck or coincidence were often blamed on witches. People on the edge of society were easy targets, especially unmarried women and impoverished widows who lacked the support of men: in 270 witchcraft trials in Elizabethan courts, 247 of the defendants were women.[2]

Accusations of witchcraft could be based on the slightest evidence, such as someone falling ill shortly after an altercation with an unmarried woman. People with little income in rural areas might forage for food and gather local plants to be used medicinally, but such knowledge could be read as a dangerous sign. A pet kept for company could be interpreted as a witch's 'familiar' (a demon in animal form); illnesses or deformities could be seen as signs of being a witch.

Shakespeare drew on these popular ideas in his portrayal of the three witches in *Macbeth*. In Act 1, Scene 3, the First Witch celebrates her revenge over a woman who has refused to give her food; in Act 4 Scene 1, the list of ingredients in their bubbling cauldron includes 'hemlock' and 'yew' (both poisonous) as well as disgusting animal and body parts (lines 5–37). The witches also take their cue for their spell-making from their familiars – a cat, a hedgehog and a harpy (a mythical creature, part woman, part bird of prey). Shakespeare also indicates that the witches do not fit conventional ideas of feminine beauty, with 'skinny lips' and 'beards' (Act 1, Scene 3, lines 45–46).

Kingship

James VI of Scotland was made King James I of England in a smooth succession after Queen Elizabeth I's death in 1603, as she left no heir. The idea of succession is central to *Macbeth*, where the king is murdered and his successor has to flee, allowing the murderer, Macbeth, to claim the Scottish throne. It was believed that James was descended from Banquo, and Shakespeare refers to this in the Apparitions scene with the '*Show of eight Kings*' (Act 4, Scene 1, line 109). Shakespeare appears to be making a clever political move in showing James's royal bloodline. Why might this be important to James, who was a distant relative of Queen Elizabeth rather than a direct descendant? (Consider that the idea of succession did not exist in Scotland in Macbeth's time.)

It was James I himself who established the idea that monarchs were divinely appointed to rule, so although the idea would not have been applicable at the time the play is set, in 11th-century Scotland, it was very relevant at the time of the play's performance, in early 17th-century England. Notice how Shakespeare balances the different traditions in the play: Duncan needs to announce his successor in Act 1, Scene 4 because Malcolm, despite being Duncan's elder son, would not necessarily assume the kingship. Could Macbeth be a possible candidate? Yet Macbeth also refers to the divine anger that could follow Duncan's murder, suggesting that he sees Duncan as God's appointed ruler.

Masculinity and femininity

Definitions of masculinity and femininity were much debated in Shakespeare's time, and he explores these ideas and expectations in *Macbeth*.

Macbeth is a candidate for kingship because he has shown himself to be an impressive soldier and leader. The Sergeant at the beginning of the play refers to 'brave Macbeth' (Act 1, Scene 2, line 16), and Duncan calls him a 'worthy gentleman', giving him honours (Act 1, Scene 2, line 24). In the brutal, warring world, men are praised for their bravery and military skill.

Later in the play, Macbeth voices his fears that murdering his king would be too brutal an act, saying, 'I dare do all that may become a man' (Act 1, Scene 7, line 46); in contrast, Lady Macbeth argues that the murder would make him 'so much more the man' (line 51). While Macduff is reeling at the news of his family's slaughter, Malcolm instructs him to 'Dispute it like a man' by fighting (Act 4, Scene 3, line 220); Macduff's response is, 'I must also feel it as a man' (Act 4, Scene 3, line 221), suggesting that compassion and grief is also part of manhood.

Elizabeth I was an independent female monarch who refused to marry, yet during her reign women did not have the same rights to property, wealth and political power as men. Women were expected to be obedient to masculine authority and ready to nurture children. It could be argued that Shakespeare's characterisation of Lady Macbeth challenges these gender assumptions. Consider, for example, how she persuades Macbeth to carry out Duncan's murder: is Shakespeare suggesting that she is more ambitious and ruthless than her husband?

In Act 1, Scene 5, Lady Macbeth delivers her famous soliloquy, where she calls on spirits to 'unsex' her and fill her 'from the crown to the toe, top-full / Of direst cruelty' (lines 42–43); she asks for her nurturing 'milk' to be removed from her 'woman's breasts' and replaced with 'gall' (lines 47–48). In this way, Shakespeare overturns ideals of maternal femininity. Later in Act 1, she contrasts Macbeth's infirmity with her own determination, and makes the shocking suggestion that she would have 'pluck'd my nipple from [the] boneless gums' of a 'smiling' baby and 'dash'd the brains out' had she 'sworn' to have done so (Act 1, Scene 7, lines 55–58). What do these lines suggest about Lady Macbeth?

Yet Shakespeare's characterisation is seldom simple. Perhaps the fact that Lady Macbeth has to call on the help of 'spirits' and 'murd'ring ministers' to 'unsex' her (Act 1, Scene 5, lines 40–48) implies that she recognises her instinctive compassion could weaken her ambition. Is her speech about dashing the baby's brains out simply rhetoric to persuade Macbeth, rather than an action she would – or could – commit? Shakespeare provides a number of clues about Lady Macbeth's hidden vulnerability. Consider, for example, her inability to kill Duncan because, she says, he 'resembled / My father as he slept' (Act 2, Scene 2, lines 12–13) and the sleepwalking scene, where Lady Macbeth tries to wash her hands of the 'damned spot' of blood (Act 5, Scene 1, line 32).

Writing, dramatic structure and techniques
Patterns of language and imagery

Shakespeare often reflects the main concerns of his plays by repeating strands of language and imagery. In *Macbeth*, where there is a clear interest in the supernatural; there are many references to light and dark and the opposition between heaven and hell, for example.

Disease imagery appears frequently, reflecting Macbeth's corruption of the natural order by killing Duncan. At times, Shakespeare links the language to stage action, as when Lady Macbeth excuses Macbeth's strange reactions to Banquo's ghost by arguing that his behaviour is the symptom of illness, something Macbeth himself calls a 'strange infirmity' (Act 3, Scene 4, line 86). Later, Macbeth himself is seen to be the disease affecting Scotland: Malcolm describes the rebels' 'great revenge' as 'med'cines' (Act 4, Scene 3, line 214).[3] The idea of disease is also made vividly clear by the appearance of a doctor in Lady Macbeth's sleepwalking scene. 'This disease is beyond my practice,' he says, recognising mental rather than physical illness (Act 5, Scene 1, line 53). Macbeth later asks him, 'Canst thou not minister to a mind diseas'd?' (Act 5, Scene 3, line 40); the doctor replies 'the patient / Must minister to himself' (lines 45–46).

Try yourself to trace out and consider the effects of other language patterns in the play, such as the balance of light and dark and the religious imagery mentioned above.

Soliloquies and psychology

A soliloquy is a speech delivered by a character, usually alone on stage. Playwrights use soliloquy to give the audience a direct insight into the character's mind, revealing their thoughts, motives and intentions. The soliloquies in *Macbeth* show that Shakespeare is interested in presenting a detailed examination of the psychology of the murderer, exploring his fears, doubts and guilt.

We can see how Shakespeare charts Macbeth's psychological state through his soliloquies, and by following them, we can recognise the stages in the tragic fall of a powerful, respected man. In his first soliloquy, Macbeth argues through a logical series of reasons why he should not murder Duncan, which lead him to conclude 'We will proceed no further in this business' (Act 1, Scene 7, line 31), before Lady Macbeth persuades him otherwise. Observe the disturbing imagery of blood and natural disorder in his second soliloquy in Act 2; how does Shakespeare show that Macbeth's rationality has declined? Consider, for example, his description of the dagger as a 'false creation' of the 'heat-oppressed brain' (Act 2, Scene 1, lines 38–39). Having committed the crime, Macbeth's soliloquy in Act 3 shows he has become more pragmatic, though he admits the death of Duncan has 'Put rancours in the vessel of my peace' (Act 3, Scene 1, line 65). By Act 5, that peace is much reduced: Macbeth laments, 'I have liv'd long enough' (Act 5, Scene 3, line 22), and regrets that his actions have robbed him of 'honour, love, obedience, troops of friends' (line 25). Macbeth's 'To-morrow' speech in Act 5, Scene 5⁴ is bleak, ending with a damning metaphor for life: 'it is a tale / Told by an idiot, full of sound and fury, / Signifying nothing' (Act 5, Scene 5, lines 26–28).

Structure

The traditional structure of Elizabethan and Jacobean drama develops the action over five acts. Shakespeare shapes that structure in *Macbeth* very skilfully. The pace through Act 1, for example, is rapid, helped by a sequence of short scenes. The audience meets the witches in the first scene, they meet Macbeth in the third, and by the end of the Act, preparations have been made for Duncan's murder. The murder itself is carried out in Act 2, Scene 2, so the mainspring of the play's action happens very quickly. While Shakespeare does examine Macbeth's character before the murder of Duncan, this structure shows that his primary interest is in Macbeth after the murder and in the psychological effects of such a deed.

Shakespeare places Macbeth's political high point – his coronation celebration – close to the centre of the play (Act 3, Scene 1), which also marks the beginning of his downfall. How does Macbeth's return to the witches in Act 4, Scene 1 show this? The three apparitions seem to confirm Macbeth's invincibility, but bear in mind the witches are 'imperfect speakers' (Act 1, Scene 3, line 70).

Act 4, Scene 3 is the only scene that takes place outside of Scotland; set in England, it is by far the play's longest scene, at 240 lines. Much of it focuses on Malcolm and Macduff testing each other. Why do you think Shakespeare devotes so much time to this? How might an audience respond to Malcolm's list of kingly virtues: 'justice, verity, temp'rance, stableness, / Bounty, perseverance, mercy, lowliness, / Devotion, patience, courage, fortitude' (lines 92–94)?

Consider also the very fast-paced final Act, with eight scenes occupying about one and a half times as many lines as Act 4, Scene 3. What effects does Shakespeare create by alternating between Macbeth's castle and the rebels before Macbeth's death?

Interpreting the play

Scholars and directors have interpreted *Macbeth* in different ways over time, showing there is no one set reading or interpretation of the play. You may find it useful to watch key scenes from different stage and film versions online and make comparisons.

The witches

Are the witches the 'Instruments of darkness' (Act 1, Scene 3, line 124) that Banquo believes them to be? It is easy to see them as purposefully manipulating Macbeth. They greet him directly three times in Act 1, Scene 3, and by calling him 'Thane of Cawdor' and predicting that he 'shalt be King hereafter' (lines 49–50) they appear to have supernatural knowledge. The witches seem to know the future, but is that the same as creating it? It is Macbeth, not the witches, who arrives at the 'horrid image' of 'murder' (Act 1, Scene 3, lines 135 and 139).

Despite Macbeth's and Banquo's clear physical descriptions of the witches, few modern productions have based their witches on these. The 1976 RSC production, of the performances listed here, was the closest to Shakespeare's ideas, as it was contextually accurate. The production depicted the witches as marginalised women, one of them suffering from mental impairment, who used crude puppets for the apparitions. In two recent RSC versions of *Macbeth*, the witches were played by children, highlighting the importance of children and childlessness in the play. Perhaps more unnerving were the nurse witches in the 2007 Gielgud Theatre production, who killed the Sergeant after his speech rather than giving him treatment. Interestingly, none of these productions made clear whether the witches are responsible for events in the play or merely predict them.

Macbeth and Lady Macbeth

This husband and wife pairing is one of the most formidable in all of Shakespeare's plays. Who is the more powerful – the fierce soldier or his plotting wife? Actors have produced some fascinating interpretations of the relationship and its dynamics.

Patrick Stewart in 2007 played Macbeth as a ruthless but loyal soldier who is transformed into a monster. Christopher Ecclestone, for the RSC in 2018, played him as such a straightforward soldier that he accidentally smeared Duncan with battlefield blood on greeting him; he showed his ambition by stepping forward when Duncan announced he was appointing his successor, awkwardly stepping back when Malcolm was named.

Many actors show Lady Macbeth using her sexuality to control Macbeth. This was a key element of Kate Fleetwood's

2007 stage performance opposite Patrick Stewart, and an important part of Ian McKellen and Judi Dench's performances for the RSC in 1976. Niamh Cusack[5] and Anne-Marie Duff[6] showed Lady Macbeth losing control of her mind as she became isolated from Macbeth after Duncan's murder. How might such interpretations affect our view of her character?

Is peace restored?

At the end of the play, Malcolm strikes an optimistic note: he promises to reward his loyal supporters and call home those forced to flee during Macbeth's rule. These acts, he says, will be performed 'in measure, time and place' (Act 5, Scene 8, line 73). Malcolm then turns his thoughts towards his coronation. The disorder of Macbeth's regime is over; however, we might wonder whether the play's action convinces us that Malcolm is right.

Macbeth starts with a violent battle for the throne and ends in the same way. At the beginning, Macbeth's acts of barbarity are praised; at the end, the death of Siward's son's is celebrated because he died fighting. When Malcolm suggests that Siward's son is 'worth more sorrow' (Act 5, Scene 8, line 50), Siward shows military values by denying it: 'He's worth no more. / They say he parted well and paid his score' (lines 51–52). As Marilyn French observes, 'although some balance is restored to the kingdom, there is no change in its value structure.'[7] In *Macbeth*, Shakespeare presents a society largely ruled by warlike men, where manhood is defined by military ambition and ruthlessness. As French also says, 'Macbeth's crime is not that he is a murderer. His crime is a failure to make the distinction his culture expects among the objects of his slaughter.'[8] Malcolm needs to appear confident, but in this war-torn Scotland, with no law of succession, there may well be another rebel with murderous eyes on the throne. Shakespeare seldom gives us fully happy endings.

Shakespeare's theatre

An Elizabethan playhouse. Note the apron stage protruding into the auditorium, the space below it, the inner room at the rear of the stage, the gallery above the inner stage, the canopy over the main stage, and the absence of a roof over the audience.

William Shakespeare (1564–1616) was a man rooted in theatre. He began his career as an actor, so had an actor's sense of which speeches would be effective on stage and how plays could be delivered with maximum impact. When writing plays, he worked directly with his company, the Lord Chamberlain's Men, so it is likely that he took on board feedback from other actors.

The Globe Theatre in London, where most of Shakespeare's plays were first performed, opened in 1599. By this time, Shakespeare was a man of theatrical influence and a shareholder in The Globe. However, the idea of a permanent theatre in London was relatively new: the city's first theatre was built in 1576. Theatres were becoming an important source of entertainment, but they were also places where radical ideas were explored. Indeed, the Puritans, who began to dominate English politics from the 1630s, considered plays to be subversive and passed a law closing theatres down in September 1642.

To get a good idea of what Shakespeare's theatre was like, we can look at the new Globe Theatre, which opened in 1997 on the site of the original, on the south bank of the Thames. It was built from plans drawn from painstaking research and used Elizabethan materials and building methods, though with added safety features such as fire exits and sprinklers.

The Globe building was circular – in Shakespeare's *Henry V* it is described as a 'wooden O',[9] with a stage raised on a 'scaffold'[10] (in the modern Globe theatre, the stage is at adult chest height). The stage stuck out into the circular yard, known as the Pit, surrounded on three sides by the audience. There was probably a curtained-off area to the rear of the stage, allowing dramatic reveals, and a gallery above that was used by musicians, as well as for central scenes, such as the now-famous balcony scene in *Romeo and Juliet*.

A ticket to stand in the Pit cost a penny (about £1 in today's money) so ordinary working people could afford to attend. Audience members in the Pit were known as groundlings; a number of characters in Shakespeare's plays make disparaging remarks about them. Around the Pit, forming the walls of the theatre, were more expensive seats on three levels. Access to these seats cost at least double the entrance to the Pit, and a box in a prime position cost considerably more. Shakespeare's audiences therefore represented a full cross-section of Elizabethan society. Indeed, King James I was the patron of Shakespeare's theatre company and attended performances at court.

A thatched roof covered the seating areas and the stage, but the central Pit was open to the weather. There was no artificial lighting, so performances usually started in the early afternoon. The atmosphere at times was probably quite rowdy; the groundlings would form a lively crowd, eating and drinking during performances and voicing their opinions about the events of the play.

Productions in the theatre had very little in the way of sets, making scene changes quick and easy. Actors could descend from above or use the stage trapdoor for entrances and exits. Costumes showed little regard for historical accuracy. Wealthy patrons sometimes handed down resplendent robes to actors playing noblemen and royalty; occasionally, companies spent considerable sums on costumes; there could be rudimentary armour or improvised togas for Roman characters. Yet everything was an approximation: in *Henry V*, the Chorus appeals to the audience's imagination to make up for the lack of numbers in battle scenes, asking 'Piece out our imperfections with your thoughts'.[11]

While the visual elements in Shakespeare's plays were simple, the words held great importance. Shakespearean audiences would speak of going to *hear* a play rather than to see one (the Latin root of the word *audience* means 'to hear'). Although many audience members in the Pit would have been illiterate, England had a long tradition of oral storytelling. Listeners loved words and paid careful attention to them, which is why Shakespeare's plays are full of rich verbal imagery and extensive word play.

In Shakespeare's time, all actors were male and boys played female parts, which perhaps explains why women characters dress up as boys to disguise themselves in a number of Shakespeare's comedies, such as *Twelfth Night* and *As You Like It*. Adult comic actors probably played older comic women, such as Juliet's nurse. Actors needed a wide range of skills and were expected to be able to fence, sing, dance and play musical instruments. We know from *Hamlet*, however, that Shakespeare did not appreciate over-the-top actors spoiling his plays: Hamlet tells a group of travelling actors they should 'not saw the air too much with your hand',[12] as this would lead an actor to tear 'a passion to tatters'.[13]

The Globe was one of several London theatres, and not all of them were outdoors. Indoor theatres were lit by candles and could make use of sets, allowing designers to produce elaborate scenic designs on backcloths for plays with music known as masques. In 1608 Shakespeare's company took over the indoor Blackfriars Theatre, and Shakespeare's play *The Tempest* was first produced there. The Blackfriars' rectangular auditorium with the stage at the shorter end was a very different design.

When studying a play by Shakespeare, think how scenes might originally have been performed and how the simple stage might have been used. Consider how the cruder comic scenes would have appealed to the groundlings, at times a few inches from the actors, and how elaborate elements of a play like *The Tempest*, which includes a shipwreck in a storm and a banquet that appears and disappears, would have benefited from the facilities of the Blackfriars Theatre. By staging plays at Blackfriars and at Court, Shakespeare was also catering to a more educated, wealthy audience than the groundlings in the Pit, suggesting how widely his plays were admired.

Endnotes

1   King James VI of Scotland became King James I of England in 1603, three years before Macbeth was first performed.

2   Alchin, L.K. 'Elizabeth Witchcraft and Witches'. http://www.elizabethan-era.org.uk/elizabethan-witchcraft-and-witches.htm. Accessed 10 July 2019.

3   By contrast, the saintly English King Edward is presented as having the ability to cure a disease called 'the evil' (Act 4, Scene 3, line 146).

4   Macbeth's speech in Act 5, Scene 5 is usually regarded as a soliloquy, although Seyton is still on stage (as Macbeth's speech is not addressed to him).

5   Cusack played opposite Christopher Ecclestone in the RSC 2018 production.

6   Duff played opposite Rory Kinnear in the 2018 National Theatre production.

7   French, Marilyn. *Shakespeare's Division of Experience*, Sphere Books Ltd, 1983, p. 250.

8   Ibid, p. 243.

9   Shakespeare, William. *Complete Works of William Shakespeare*, HarperCollins Publishers, 1994, p. 590.

10   Ibid, p. 590.

11   Ibid, p. 590.

12   Ibid, p. 1101.
13   Ibid, p. 1101.

Further reading

French, M. *Shakespeare's Division of Experience*, New York, Ballantine Books, 1983.

Levin, Carole. 'Witchcraft in Shakespeare's England.' *The British Library: Discovering Literature*, 15 March 2016. https://www.bl.uk/shakespeare/articles/manhood-and-the-milk-of-human-kindness-in-macbeth

'*Macbeth*'. Royal Shakespeare Company. https://www.rsc.org.uk/macbeth/

'*Macbeth* Study Guide'. Shakespeare Online. http://www.shakespeare-online.com/plays/macbeth/macbethresources.html

Ryan, Kiernan. 'Manhood and the "milk of human kindness" in *Macbeth*.' *The British Library: Discovering Literature*, 15 March 2016. https://www.bl.uk/shakespeare/articles/manhood-and-the-milk-of-human-kindness-in-macbeth

'Shakespeare Unlocked – *Macbeth*'. BBC. https://www.bbc.com/teach/class-clips-video/english-literature--drama-gcse-shakespeare-unlocked-macbeth/zvksjhv

Smith, E. *This Is Shakespeare*, London, Pelican Books, 2019.

Wilson Knight, G. *The Wheel of Fire* London, Routledge, 2001.

Timeline

Very little indeed is known about Shakespeare's private life: the facts included here are almost the only indisputable ones. The dates of Shakespeare's plays are those on which they were first produced.

1558	Queen Elizabeth crowned.	
1561	Francis Bacon born.	
1564	Christopher Marlowe born.	William Shakespeare born, 23 April, baptised 26 April.
1566		Shakespeare's brother, Gilbert, born.
1567	Mary, Queen of Scots, deposed. James VI (later James I of England) crowned King of Scotland.	
1572	Ben Jonson born. Lord Leicester's Company (of players) licensed; later called Lord Strange's, then the Lord Chamberlain's and finally (under James), the King's Men.	
1573	John Donne born.	
1574	The Common Council of London directs that all plays and playhouses in London must be licensed.	
1576	James Burbage builds the first public playhouse, The Theatre, at Shoreditch, outside the walls of the City.	
1577	Francis Drake begins his voyage round the world (completed 1580). *Holinshed's Chronicles of England, Scotland and Ireland* published (which	

Shakespeare later used extensively).

1582		Shakespeare married to Anne Hathaway.
1583	The Queen's Company founded by royal warrant.	Shakespeare's daughter, Susanna, born.
1585		Shakespeare's twins, Hamnet and Judith, born.
1586	Sir Philip Sidney, the Elizabethan ideal 'Christian knight', poet, patron, soldier, killed at Zutphen in the Low Countries.	
1587	Mary, Queen of Scots, beheaded. Marlowe's *Tamburlaine (Part I)* first staged.	
1588	Defeat of the Spanish Armada. Marlowe's *Tamburlaine (Part II)* first staged.	
1589	Marlowe's *Jew of Malta* and Kyd's *Spanish Tragedy* (a 'revenge tragedy' and one of the most popular plays of Elizabethan times).	
1590	Spenser's *Faerie Queene* (Books I–III) published.	
1592	Marlowe's *Doctor Faustus* and *Edward II* first staged. Witchcraft trials in Scotland. Robert Greene, a rival playwright, refers to Shakespeare as 'an upstart crow' and 'the only Shake-scene in a country'.	*Titus Andronicus* *Henry VI, Parts I, II and III* *Richard III*
1593	London theatres closed by the plague. Christopher Marlowe killed in a Deptford tavern.	*Two Gentlemen of Verona* *Comedy of Errors* *The Taming of the Shrew* *Love's Labour's Lost*
1594	Shakespeare's company becomes The Lord Chamberlain's Men.	

1595	Raleigh's first expedition to Guiana. Last expedition of Drake and Hawkins (both died).	*Romeo and Juliet* *Richard II* *A Midsummer Night's Dream*
1596	Spenser's *Faerie Queene* (Books IV–VI) published. James Burbage buys rooms at Blackfriars and begins to convert them into a theatre.	*King John* *The Merchant of Venice* Shakespeare's son Hamnet dies. Shakespeare's father is granted a coat of arms.
1597	James Burbage dies. His son Richard, a famous actor, turns the Blackfriars Theatre into a private playhouse.	*Henry IV (Part I)* Shakespeare buys and redecorates New Place at Stratford.
1598	Death of Philip II of Spain.	*Henry IV (Part II)* *Much Ado About Nothing*
1599	Death of Edmund Spenser. The Globe Theatre completed at Bankside by Richard and Cuthbert Burbage.	*Henry V* *Julius Caesar* *As You Like It*
1600	Fortune Theatre built at Cripplegate. East India Company founded for the extension of English trade and influence in the East. The Children of the Chapel begin to use the hall at Blackfriars.	*Merry Wives of Windsor* *Troilus and Cressida*
1601		*Hamlet*
1602	Sir Thomas Bodley's library opened at Oxford.	*Twelfth Night*
1603	Death of Queen Elizabeth. James I comes to the throne. Shakespeare's company becomes The King's Men. Raleigh tried, condemned and sent to the Tower.	
1604	Treaty of peace with Spain.	*Measure for Measure* *Othello* *All's Well that Ends Well*
1605	The Gunpowder Plot: an attempt by a group of Catholics to blow up the Houses of Parliament.	

1606	Guy Fawkes and other plotters executed.	*Macbeth* *King Lear*
1607	Virginia, in America, colonised. A great frost in England.	*Antony and Cleopatra* *Timon of Athens* *Coriolanus* Shakespeare's daughter, Susanna, married to Dr John Hall.
1608	The company of the Children of the Chapel Royal (who had performed at Blackfriars for ten years) is disbanded. John Milton born. Notorious pirates executed in London.	Richard Burbage leases the Blackfriars Theatre to six of his fellow actors, including Shakespeare. *Pericles, Prince of Tyre*
1609		Shakespeare's Sonnets published.
1610	A great drought in England	*Cymbeline*
1611	Chapman completes his great translation of the *Iliad*, the story of Troy. Authorised Version of the Bible published.	*A Winter's Tale* *The Tempest*
1612	Webster's *The White Devil* first staged.	Shakespeare's brother, Gilbert, dies.
1613	Globe theatre burnt down during a performance of *Henry VIII* (the firing of small cannon set fire to the thatched roof). Webster's *Duchess of Malfi* first staged.	*Henry VIII* *Two Noble Kinsmen* Shakespeare buys a house at Blackfriars.
1614	Globe Theatre rebuilt in 'far finer manner than before'.	
1616	Ben Jonson publishes his plays in one volume. Raleigh released from the Tower in order to prepare an expedition to the gold mines of Guiana.	Shakespeare's daughter, Judith, marries Thomas Quiney. Death of Shakespeare on his birthday, 23 April.
1618	Raleigh returns to England and is executed on the charge for which he was imprisoned in 1603.	
1623	Publication of the Folio edition of Shakespeare's plays.	Death of Anne Shakespeare (née Hathaway).

MACBETH

Prefatory note

This Shakespeare play uses the full Alexander text. By keeping in mind the fact that the language has changed considerably in four hundred years, as have customs, jokes, and stage conventions, the editors have aimed at helping the modern reader – whether English is their mother tongue or not – to grasp the full significance of the play. The Notes, intended primarily for examination candidates, are presented in a simple, direct style. The needs of those unfamiliar with British culture have been specially considered.

Since quiet study of the printed word is unlikely to bring fully to life plays that were written directly for the public theatre, attention has been drawn to dramatic effects which are important in performance. The editors see Shakespeare's plays as living works of art which can be enjoyed today on stage, film and television in many parts of the world.

LIST OF CHARACTERS

Duncan	King of Scotland
Malcolm *Donalbain*	} his sons
Macbeth *Banquo*	} Generals of the King's army
Macduff *Lennox* *Ross* *Menteith* *Angus* *Caithness*	} Noblemen of Scotland
Fleance	son to Banquo
Siward	Earl of Northumberland, General of the English forces
Young Siward	his son
Seyton	an officer attending on Macbeth
Boy	son to Macduff
A sergeant	
A porter	
An Old Man	
An English Doctor	
A Scots Doctor	
Lady Macbeth	
Lady Macduff	
Gentlewoman	attending on Lady Macbeth
The Weird Sisters	
Hecate	
The Ghost Of Banquo	
Apparitions	

Lords, Gentlemen, Officers, Soldiers, Murderers, Attendants and Messengers

The Scene: Scotland and England

1

ACT 1 SCENE 1

This short opening scene gives an immediate impression of mystery, horror and uncertainty. These witches would have been truly frightening to an audience in Shakespeare's day, many of whom would have seen, or at the very least known about, women burnt at the stake for selling themselves to the Devil. Macbeth is introduced by name by the Third Witch, and this raises questions in the audience's mind – who is he? And what can these disgusting hags want with him?

3. *hurlyburly* the confused noise of storm and battle. Thunder was produced for the Elizabethan stage by rolling cannon-balls. Nowadays the same effect is produced by shaking sheets of metal, or through electronic and digital sound equipment.

4. *lost and won* the first of many apparent contradictions and confusions (see line 12 of this scene). The words can mean 'decided one way or the other'.

9. *Graymalkin* a name for a grey cat, which was a common 'familiar' of witches. A familiar was a demon which attended and assisted a witch; these spirits usually took some rather sinister form.

10. *Paddock* a toad. This is the Second Witch's familiar. Sounds were probably made off-stage to represent the calls of these familiar spirits, though it is difficult to imagine what sound a toad was supposed to make.

11. *Anon!* I am coming at once.

12. This line is a kind of motto for the witches. They delight in a reversal of all the normal values. Macbeth seems to involve himself with them by echoing the phrase in Act 1, Scene 3, line 39.

13. *fog and filthy air* this may have been produced by burning resin under the stage; again, in today's theatre if an effect is required it is more likely to be produced by smoke machine, dry ice or something similar.

Osidge Library
Tel: 020 8359 3920
Email: osidge.library@barnet.gov.uk

Customer ID: *********5092**

Items that you have checked out

Title: Epic hero flop
ID: 30131057542406
Due: 08 December 2022

Title: Incredible rescue mission
ID: 30131057285378
Due: 08 December 2022

Title: Macbeth
ID: 30131057025576
Due: 08 December 2022

Title: The infinite
ID: 30131057396738
Due: 08 December 2022

Title: Unexpected super spy
ID: 30131057070416
Due: 08 December 2022

Title: World's greatest liar
ID: 30131055255993
Due: 08 December 2022

Total items: 6
Account balance: £9.10
17/11/2022 13.04
Checked out: 6
Overdue: 0
Hold requests: 0
Ready for collection: 0

ACT 1
Scene 1

An open place

[Thunder and lightning. Enter three WITCHES.*]*

First Witch
    When shall we three meet again?
    In thunder, lightning, or in rain?
Second Witch
    When the hurlyburly's done,
    When the battle's lost and won.
Third Witch
    That will be ere the set of sun.   5
First Witch
    Where the place?
Second Witch
    Upon the heath.
Third Witch
    There to meet with Macbeth.
First Witch
    I come, Graymalkin.
Second Witch
    Paddock calls.   10
Third Witch
    Anon!
All
    Fair is foul, and foul is fair:
    Hover through the fog and filthy air.

*[*WITCHES *vanish.]*

SCENE 2

The second scene deals mainly with the report of the battle in which the 'Macbeth' we have already heard about, and another man, Banquo, have excelled. However, the feeling of uncertainty is maintained, because the outcome of the battle is left in doubt by the Sergeant. He nevertheless presents Macbeth as the decisive factor, and Ross gives the same impression from his point of view when he provides the final news that the battle has been won. We get a remarkable picture of Macbeth as a kind of superman, a fearless, ferocious, almost untouchable champion of right against treachery.

1–3. *He can report ... state* He looks as though he has come, wounded, straight from the battle, and will be able to give us an up-to-date report.

5. *'Gainst my captivity* to save me from being captured.
6. *knowledge of the broil* news of the battle.

9. *choke their art* (the two exhausted swimmers) prevent each other from using their swimming skill.
10. *to that* to that end, i.e. to show that he is without doubt a traitor.
12. *swarm upon him* like lice.
12. *Western Isles* islands to the west, including Ireland and the Hebrides.
13. *kerns and gallowglasses* lightly-armed foot-soldiers and horsemen armed with axes.
14–15. *Fortune* the Roman goddess Fortuna, regarded as highly unreliable. Macbeth ignores her (***Disdaining Fortune,*** line 17) and takes his fate into his own hands, a trait we are to see repeated later in the play.
17–18. *brandished steel ... execution* His sword steamed with the hot blood of those he had just killed.
19. *valour's minion* the favourite of Valour (personified in much the same way as Fortune).
carv'd out his passage cut his way through the men on the battlefield.
22–3. *Till he unseam'd ...* he thrust his sword in at the navel (nave), ripped him open up to the jaws (chaps), then cut his head off and stuck it on the battlements.

Scene 2

A camp near Forres

[Alarum within. Enter KING DUNCAN, MALCOLM,
DONALBAIN, LENNOX *with* ATTENDANTS, *meeting a
bleeding* SERGEANT.*]*

Duncan

What bloody man is that? He can report,
As seemeth by his plight, of the revolt
The newest state.

Malcolm

This is the sergeant
Who like a good and hardy soldier fought
'Gainst my captivity. Hail, brave friend!   5
Say to the King the knowledge of the broil
As thou didst leave it.

Sergeant

Doubtful it stood,
As two spent swimmers that do cling together
And choke their art. The merciless Macdonwald –
Worthy to be a rebel, for to that   10
The multiplying villainies of nature
Do swarm upon him – from the Western Isles
Of kerns and gallowglasses is supplied;
And Fortune, on his damned quarrel smiling,
Show'd like a rebel's whore. But all's too weak;   15
For brave Macbeth – well he deserves that name –
Disdaining Fortune, with his brandish'd steel
Which smok'd with bloody execution,
Like valour's minion, carv'd out his passage
Till he fac'd the slave;   20
Which ne'er shook hands, nor bade farewell to him,
Till he unseam'd him from the nave to th' chaps,
And fix'd his head upon our battlements.

24. *cousin* Macbeth and Duncan were both grandsons of King Malcolm, but in any case the word cousin was often used by sovereigns of their noblemen.

24. *worthy gentleman!* What Macbeth has just done seems hardly gentlemanly, but there is no irony in Duncan's remark. Such actions in defence of king and country would have been regarded as truly to be admired.

25–8. *As whence ... Discomfort swells* 'Just as storms fatal to ships can burst out of the east, where the sun first shines, so danger springs from the place where everything seems well.' Note the irony here, even if the Sergeant doesn't realize it. These words could be a warning to Duncan about Macbeth, who seems fair.

30. *Compell'd ... heels* Forced these unreliable soldiers to rely on running away.

31. *Norweyan* an old form of Norwegian.

31. *surveying vantage* seeing his chance. No doubt Duncan's troops had relaxed on seeing the kerns run away.

32. *With furbished arms* 'having repaired their weapons' (or perhaps taken up new ones).

34–5. *Yes ... the lion* The Sergeant is being very sarcastic. 'Yes, they were about as dismayed as an eagle is by a sparrow, or a lion by a hare,' he says.

36. *sooth* truth.

37. *as cannons ... cracks* Like cannons with double charges of gunpowder.

39–40. *Except they meant ... Golgotha* Unless they intended to bathe in the steaming wounds (of their enemies) or make the battle as grimly memorable a scene as the crucifixion of Christ.

43–4. *So well ... both* Your words and your wounds do you equal honour.

44. *smack* taste.

45. *Thane* a Scottish nobleman and landowner, often the chief of a clan

47. *So should he ... strange* His appearance suggests that he has strange news to tell.

Duncan
  O valiant cousin! worthy gentleman!
Sergeant
  As whence the sun gins his reflection   25
  Shipwrecking storms and direful thunders break,
  So from that spring whence comfort seem'd to come
  Discomfort swells. Mark, King of Scotland, mark:
  No sooner justice had, with valour arm'd,
  Compell'd these skipping kerns to trust their heels,   30
  But the Norweyan lord, surveying vantage,
  With furbish'd arms and new supplies of men,
  Began a fresh assault.
Duncan
                  Dismay'd not this
  Our captains, Macbeth and Banquo?
Sergeant
                      Yes;
  As sparrows eagles, or the hare the lion.   35
  If I say sooth, I must report they were
  As cannons overcharg'd with double cracks;
  So they doubly redoubled strokes upon the foe.
  Except they meant to bathe in reeking wounds,
  Or memorize another Golgotha,   40
  I cannot tell –
  But I am faint; my gashes cry for help.
Duncan
  So well thy words become thee as thy wounds;
  They smack of honour both. – Go get him surgeons.

     [Exit SERGEANT, *attended. Enter* ROSS.*]*

  Who comes here?
Malcolm
              The worthy Thane of Ross.   45
Lennox
  What a haste looks through his eyes!
  So should he look that seems to speak things strange.

50–1. *Where ... cold* Where the Norwegian banners mock the (Scottish) sky and, as they wave, freeze our men with fear.

52. *Norway himself* King Sweno of Norway.

54. *a dismal conflict* one which filled the Scottish forces with foreboding.

55. *Bellona's bridegroom* the bridegroom of Bellona, the Roman goddess of war. Macbeth is being compared with Mars, the god of war himself.

55. *lapp'd in proof* wearing tried and tested armour.

56. *Confronted ... self-comparisons* Gave him something (i.e. a model of a fighting man) to compare himself with.

58. *Curbing his lavish spirit* overcoming his insolent courage.

61. *craves composition* begs for peace terms.

62. *Nor would we ... men* We would not allow him to bury his dead soldiers.

63. *disbursed* paid.

63. *Saint Colme's Inch* a small island in the Firth of Forth, now called Inchcolm. (St Colme is another form of St Columba.)

64. *dollars* These coins were in fact not minted until the early sixteenth century, 500 years after the time of the real Duncan and Macbeth. Does it matter that Shakespeare isn't worried about such inaccuracy? Could it have had a deliberate purpose?

65–6. *deceive ... interest* treacherously attack our dearest interests.
pronounce his present death order his immediate execution.

Ross
God save the King!
Duncan
Whence cam'st thou, worthy thane?
Ross
                              From Fife, great King
Where the Norweyan banners flout the sky   50
And fan our people cold.
Norway himself, with terrible numbers,
Assisted by that most disloyal traitor
The Thane of Cawdor, began a dismal conflict,
Till that Bellona's bridegroom, lapp'd in proof,   55
Confronted him with self-comparisons,
Point against point rebellious, arm 'gainst arm,
Curbing his lavish spirit; and to conclude,
The victory fell on us.
Duncan
                    Great happiness!
Ross
That now   60
Sweno, the Norways' king, craves composition;
Nor would we deign him burial of his men
Till he disbursed, at Saint Colme's Inch,
Ten thousand dollars to our general use.
Duncan
No more that Thane of Cawdor shall deceive   65
Our bosom interest. Go pronounce his present death,
And with his former title greet Macbeth.
Ross
I'll see it done.
Duncan
What be hath lost, noble Macbeth hath won.

[Exeunt.]

SCENE 3

The meeting of Macbeth and the witches, which we heard them predict in Act 1, Scene 1, is about to take place. However, before Macbeth arrives on the heath, unaware of what he will find, the witches plan to torment a sea-captain whose wife has annoyed them.

2. *Killing swine* Witches were said to kill farm animals, often in revenge for some supposed insult.

7. *Aroint thee ... !* Get out!

7. *rump-fed* this probably means 'fed on rump-steak', therefore sleek and plump. The gaunt witches would envy her.

7. *ronyon* worthless woman.

8. *Tiger* a common name for a ship in Shakespeare's time.

9. There are records of criminal trials in which so-called witches confessed that they went to sea in a sieve.

10. Another special ability witches were belived to have was to turn themselves into animals, but when they did this they became tailless and could be identified.

11. She seems almost fuming with rage and malice. What do you think she intends to do?

15–18. *I myself have ... card* 'I have control of all the other winds and (I know) the exact harbours from which they blow, from all points of the compass.' The main point is that she wants to prevent the *Tiger* from entering any port, and leave the poor ship miserably tossing on the waves.

19. Because the *Tiger* will not be able to refill her water-supply.

20–1. This is an ominous suggestion of Macbeth's later insomnia (see, for example, Act 3, Scene 4, line 141).

21. *pent-house lid* An eyelid slopes something like the roof of a pent-house. (A penthouse is a small structure built against a larger one, therefore having only one roof-slope).

22. *forbid* cursed.

23. *sev'nights* weeks. Compare the similar word fortnight (fourteen nights) which is still in regular use. The witch is going to manipulate the winds to keep the ship at sea for 81 weeks.

Scene 3

A blasted heath

[Thunder. Enter the three WITCHES.]

First Witch
Where hast thou been, sister?
Second Witch
Killing swine.
Third Witch
Sister, where thou?
First Witch
A sailor's wife had chestnuts in her lap,
And mounch'd, and mounch'd, and mounch'd.　　　　5
'Give me' quoth I.
'Aroint thee, witch!' the rump-fed ronyon cries.
Her husband's to Aleppo gone, master o' th' Tiger;
But in a sieve I'll thither sail
And, like a rat without a tail,　　　　10
I'll do, I'll do, and I'll do.
Second Witch
I'll give thee a wind,
First Witch
Th'art kind.
Third Witch
And I another.
First Witch
I myself have all the other;　　　　15
And the very ports they blow,
All the quarters that they know
I' th' shipman's card.
I'll drain him dry as hay:
Sleep shall neither night nor day　　　　20
Hang upon his pent-house lid;
He shall live a man forbid;
Weary sev'nights, nine times nine,

24. *dwindle, peak* become thin.

25. *bark* ship. It is important to note that the power of the witches is limited. At crucial points in the play Macbeth excuses or explains his past actions or what he is about to do by assuming that they have absolute power and knowledge, but this is not so.

29. *a pilot's thumb.* Bits of dead bodies were valued ingredients in making spells.

31. Is this perhaps a supernatural drum? There is no indication that Macbeth and Banquo have an escort, but they may have.

32. *Weird* This coms from an Old English word 'wyrd' which means fate.

33. *Posters* creatures which travel quickly.

35–6. Three and multiples of three have always been regarded as magic numbers. At this point they also indicate roughly the steps of their dance: 'three paces your way, three paces my way, and three more paces (in the direction of the Third Witch).'

37. *wound up* 'set, and ready for action'. At this very moment Macbeth and Banquo enter, as though brought there by the charm.

38. *So foul and fair* Macbeth's unconscious echo of the witches' words in Act 1, Scene 1, confirms the impression that he is already under their influence.

39. *How far is't called … ?* How far do they reckon it is …?

39–61. Banquo's reaction to the first sight of the witches is a suspicious one. Macbeth says little, but seems far more prepared than Banquo to accept the witches' words.

42–3. *aught that man may question?* beings with whom one is allowed to communicate?

44. *choppy* chapped. The fact that the witches put their fingers on their lips in answer to Banquo seems to suggest that they want to speak, not to him, but to Macbeth.

Shall he dwindle, peak, and pine.
Though his bark cannot be lost,   25
Yet it shall be tempest-tost.
Look what I have.
Second Witch
Show me, show me.
First Witch
Here I have a pilot's thumb,
Wreck'd as homeward he did come.   30

[Drum within.]

Third Witch
A drum, a drum! Macbeth doth come.
All
The Weird Sisters, hand in hand,
Posters of the sea and land,
Thus do go about, about;
Thrice to thine, and thrice to mine,   35
And thrice again, to make up nine.
Peace! The charm's wound up.

[Enter MACBETH and BANQUO.]

Macbeth
So foul and fair a day I have not seen.
Banquo
How far is't call'd to Forres? What are these,
So withered, and so wild in their attire,   40
That look not like th' inhabitants o' th' earth,
And yet are on't? Live you, or are you aught
That man may question? You seem to understand me,
By each at once her choppy finger laying
Upon her skinny lips. You should be women,   45
And yet your beards forbid me to interpret
That you are so.
Macbeth
                    Speak, if you can. What are you?

13

50. *hereafter* in the future. They have just addressed him as the present Thane of Cawdor, as well as Glamis.

51. Banquo notices that Macbeth jumps when he hears the witches' greetings. Is this just normal surprise and wonder, or has Macbeth already considered the possibility of becoming king, by foul means if necessary?

53. *fantastical* imaginary.

53–4. *or that … ye show?* or are you what you appear to be?

55–6. *present grace* being Thane of Glamis.

great prediction Of noble having becoming Thane of Cawdor.

royal hope becoming king.

57. *rapt withal* entranced by them (the witches' mysterious greetings).

58. *look into the seeds of time* Banquo is prepared to accept the witches' power to see into the future, but he goes on to show (lines 60–1) that he will not put himself in their power. Their response is to speak to him in riddles, whereas they gave Macbeth plain statements.

67. *get kings*: be the ancestor of kings.

70. *imperfect speakers* Macbeth says this because he wants to know more. He has come out of his trance and now demands further information.

71. *Sinel* Macbeth's father, from whom he had inherited the title of Thane of Glamis.

73–4. Neither Macbeth nor Banquo seems to have heard of Cawdor's treachery.

First Witch
    All hail, Macbeth! Hail to thee. Thane of Glamis!
Second Witch
    All hail, Macbeth! Hail to thee. Thane of Cawdor!
Third Witch
    All hail, Macbeth, that shalt be King hereafter!   50
Banquo
    Good sir, why do you start, and seem to fear
    Things that do sound so fair? I' th' name of truth,
    Are ye fantastical, or that indeed
    Which outwardly ye show? My noble partner
    You greet with present grace and great prediction   55
    Of noble having and of royal hope,
    That he seems rapt withal. To me you speak not.
    If you can look into the seeds of time
    And say which grain will grow and which will not,
    Speak then to me, who neither beg nor fear   60
    Your favours nor your hate.
First Witch
    Hail!
Second Witch
    Hail!
Third Witch
    Hail!
First Witch
    Lesser than Macbeth, and greater.   65
Second Witch
    Not so happy, yet much happier.
Third Witch
    Thou shalt get kings, though thou be none.
    So, all hail, Macbeth and Banquo!
First Witch
    Banquo and Macbeth, all hail!
Macbeth
    Stay, you imperfect speakers, tell me more.   70
    By Sinel's death I know I am Thane of Glamis;
    But how of Cawdor? The Thane of Cawdor lives,

74. *Stands not ... belief* Is so unlikely as to be unbelievable.

76. *owe* own, possess.

intelligence information.

78. Having asked for information twice, Macbeth becomes bolder and orders the witches to answer him.

79–80. The witches have vanished like burst bubbles. Although they had seemed very real, physical, living creatures, it now appears that they belong to the supernatural.

81. *corporal* made of flesh and blood.

84–5. *the insane root ... prisoner* the root (of the hemlock or some other plant) which causes madness when eaten.

86. Is Macbeth envious and annoyed because no mention was made of his own heirs?

91. *Thy personal ... fight* Your individual contribution in putting down the rebellion of Macdonwald.

95. Ross goes on to mention the other phase of the battle, against the Norwegian forces.

95. *stout* bold, tough.

A prosperous gentleman; and to be King
Stands not within the prospect of belief,
No more than to be Cawdor. Say from whence   75
You owe this strange intelligence, or why
Upon this blasted heath you stop our way
With such prophetic greeting? Speak, I charge you.

[WITCHES vanish.]

Banquo
    The earth hath bubbles, as the water has,
    And these are of them. Whither are they vanish'd?   80
Macbeth
    Into the air; and what seem'd corporal melted
    As breath into the wind. Would they had stay'd!
Banquo
    Were such things here as we do speak about?
    Or have we eaten on the insane root
    That takes the reason prisoner?   85
Macbeth
    Your children shall be kings.
Banquo
                    You shall be King.
Macbeth
    And Thane of Cawdor too; went it not so?
Banquo
    To th' self-same tune and words. Who's here?

[Enter ROSS and ANGUS.]

Ross
    The King hath happily receiv'd, Macbeth,
    The news of thy success; and when he reads   90
    Thy personal venture in the rebels' fight,
    His wonders and his praises do contend
    Which should be thine or his. Silenc'd with that,
    In viewing o'er the rest o' th' self-same day,
    He finds thee in the stout Norweyan ranks,   95

96–7. *Nothing afeard … death* Ross comments that Macbeth is not frightened by the sight of the mangled bodies of those he has killed. We will see a different reaction later.

97–100. Macbeth's great achievement was acclaimed in all the messages which piled up in front of Duncan. It is especially ironic that just when the audience is beginning to suspect Macbeth's intentions, everyone else on stage is praising him.

98. *post with post* message after message.

102. *herald … sight* escort you into the king's presence.

104. *for an earnest* as a first instalment.

105–6. The words are close enough to those of the Second Witch to underline the rapid fulfilment of the prophecy.

106. *addition* title.

107. Banquo has clearly decided that the witches are evil.

108–9. The play contains many examples of imagery related to clothes, particularly those that do not fit. This creates a picture of Macbeth wearing clothes that were not meant for him. Keep this in mind as the play develops.

110–11. The ex-thane of Cawdor is under sentence of death (see Act 1, Scene 2, line 66).

111. *was combin'd* allied himself.

112. *line the rebel* assist Macdonwald.

113. *hidden help and vantage* secret aid.

114. *labour'd … wreck* worked to ruin his country.

115. *treasons capital* acts of treason worthy of the death penalty.

117. *The greatest is behind* the fulfilment of the Third Witch's prophecy, the Kingship, will follow after this stage, in the future (hence the word 'behind').

118. Macbeth again refers to the prophecy about Banquo's children becoming kings.

Nothing afeard of what thyself didst make,
Strange images of death. As thick as tale
Came post with post, and every one did bear
Thy praises in his kingdom's great defence,
And pour'd them down before him.

Angus

We are sent   100
To give thee, from our royal master, thanks;
Only to herald thee into his sight,
Not pay thee.

Ross

And, for an earnest of a greater honour,
He bade me, from him, call thee Thane of Cawdor;   105
In which addition, hail, most worthy Thane!
For it is thine.

Banquo

What, can the devil speak true?

Macbeth

The Thane of Cawdor lives; why do you dress me
In borrowed robes?

Angus

Who was the Thane lives yet;
But under heavy judgment bears that life   110
Which he deserves to lose. Whether he was combin'd
With those of Norway, or did line the rebel
With hidden help and vantage, or that with both
He labour'd in his country's wreck, I know not;
But treasons capital, confess'd and prov'd,   115
Have overthrown him.

Macbeth

[aside]   Glamis, and Thane of Cawdor!
The greatest is behind. – Thanks for your pains.
[Aside to BANQUO*]* Do you not hope your children
        shall be kings,
When those that gave the Thane of Cawdor to me
Promis'd no less to them?

19

120. *trusted home* believed in fully.

122–6. Banquo reveals his own deep distrust of the witches and their words, saying 'The Devil's helpers often impress us and win our confidence by telling us some small truths about our lives so that, once we are in their power, they can deceive us in really important matters (and thus destroy us).'

128–9. *the swelling act ... theme* Macbeth sees himself as king at the climax of a great drama.

130. *soliciting* prompting, egging on.

131–3. What Banquo suspected and dismissed (a small truth leading to betrayal *In deepest consequence)* Macbeth also suspects but will not dismiss.

134–7. *If good ... nature?* Already Macbeth is contradicting Ross's remark in lines 97–8. Here is an image of death of which he is clearly afraid. Is it one of his own creation or not? He is certainly considering murder (see line 140).

135. *unfix my hair* make my hair stand on end.

136. *seated* firmly fixed.

137. *Against the use of nature* in an unnatural way.

137–8. *Present fears ... imaginings* A real cause of fear (e.g. a fierce enemy in the recent battle) is less frightening than something horrible which you imagine.

139–42. Macbeth is obsessed by the idea of murder and is incapable of normal action. Nothing seems real to him except what he is creating in his mind.

143. *rapt* lost in his own thoughts.

144–5. At first, in order to escape his horrible imaginings, Macbeth adopts the attitude of saying to himself: 'There is no need for me to take any action; if it is my fate to be king, it will just happen that way.'

145–6. *New honours ... use* The honours which have just come to him (Macbeth) are like new clothes which take time to shape themselves comfortably to the body. Note the reference to clothing imagery again.

Banquo
  [aside to MACBETH*]*   That, trusted home,   120
  Might yet enkindle you unto the crown,
  Besides the Thane of Cawdor. But 'tis strange;
  And oftentimes to win us to our harm,
  The Instruments of darkness tell us truths,
  Win us with honest trifles, to betray's   125
  In deepest consequence. –
  Cousins, a word, I pray you.
Macbeth
  [aside]   Two truths are told,
  As happy prologues to the swelling act
  Of the imperial theme. – I thank you, gentlemen.
  [Aside] This supernatural soliciting   130
  Cannot be ill; cannot be good. If ill,
  Why hath it given me earnest of success,
  Commencing in a truth I am Thane of Cawdor.
  If good, why do I yield to that suggestion
  Whose horrid image doth unfix my hair   135
  And make my seated heart knock at my ribs
  Against the use of nature? Present fears
  Are less than horrible imaginings.
  My thought, whose murder yet is but fantastical,
  Shakes so my single state of man   140
  That function is smothered in surmise,
  And nothing is but what is not.
Banquo
  Look how our partner's rapt.
Macbeth
  [aside] If chance will have me King, why, chance
          may crown me,
  Without my stir.
Banquo
                New honours come upon him,   145
  Like our strange garments, cleave not to their mould
  But with the aid of use.

147–8. *Come what ... roughest day* Macbeth continues to shrug off his troubled thoughts: 'I suppose I shall live through it. Even the most troubled day has to come to an end.' The words give him something to hang on to.

149. Banquo indicates politely that they are waiting until Macbeth is ready to go.

150–1. 'Do forgive me. My over–tired brain was disturbed by things that I can't even remember now'. This may not seem a big lie, but it is a lie nevertheless.

151. *your pains* your services to me.

152–3. *where every day ... read them* i.e. in his mind.

155. *The interim having weigh'd it* the interval having given us a chance to consider it.

156. *Our free hearts* Can either of their hearts be described as free?

Macbeth [aside]
                    Come what come may,
  Time and the hour runs through the roughest day.

Banquo
  Worthy Macbeth, we stay upon your leisure.

Macbeth
  Give me your favour. My dull brain was wrought   150
  With things forgotten. Kind gentlemen, your pains
  Are register'd where every day I turn
  The leaf to read them. Let us toward the King.
  [Aside to BANQUO*]* Think upon what hath chanc'd;
      and, at more time,
  The interim having weigh'd it, let us speak   155
  Our free hearts each to other.

Banquo
  [aside to MACBETH*]*   Very gladly.

Macbeth
  [aside to BANQUO*]* Till then, enough. – Come, friends.

                [Exeunt.]

SCENE 4

The rebels and the foreign invaders have been defeated. King Duncan wants to celebrate his country's safety by making Malcolm, his eldest son, the official heir to the throne. It is a formal occasion, which would have been vividly presented by Shakespeare's company, the King's Men, with rich costume and all the symbols of majesty. The scene appears to stress happy, natural relationships between those present with Duncan as the warm-hearted father-king. Macbeth's apparently unexpected arrival gives Duncan further opportunity for rejoicing.

2. *Those in commission* 'the officials charged with the duty' (Ross was sent to deal with it. Act 1, Scene 2, lines 66–7).

9. *As one ... death* Like an actor perfectly trained in a death-scene.
9. *studied* learnt by heart.
10. *the dearest thing he ow'd* his life.
10. *ow'd;* owned.
11. *careless* not worth any care.
11–12. *There's no art ... face* 'There's no way of telling, from a man's face, what's going on in his mind'. At this moment Macbeth enters. Duncan has no idea that his own words could be accurately applied to his new Thane of Cawdor. This is a good example of dramatic irony.

16–18. *Thou art ... overtake thee* You are so far ahead in worth and ability that it's difficult for admiration and reward to catch up with you.
19–20. *That the proportion ... mine!* So that I could have thanked you and rewarded you according to your merit.

Scene 4

Forres. The palace

[Flourish. Enter DUNCAN, MALCOLM, DONALBAIN, LENNOX
and ATTENDANTS.*]*

Duncan
    Is execution done on Cawdor? Are not
    Those in commission yet return'd?
Malcolm
                    My liege,
    They are not yet come back. But I have spoke
    With one that saw him die; who did report
    That very frankly he confess'd his treasons,   5
    Implor'd your Highness' pardon, and set forth
    A deep repentance. Nothing in his life
    Became him like the leaving it: he died
    As one that had been studied in his death
    To throw away the dearest thing he ow'd   10
    As 'twere a careless trifle.
Duncan
                There's no art
    To find the mind's construction in the face.
    He was a gentleman on whom I built
    An absolute trust.

    [Enter MACBETH, BANQUO, ROSS *and* ANGUS.*]*

            O worthiest cousin!
    The sin of my ingratitude even now   15
    Was heavy on me. Thou art so far before
    That swiftest wing of recompense is slow
    To overtake thee. Would thou hadst less deserv'd,
    That the proportion both of thanks and payment
    Might have been mine! Only I have left to say,   20
    More is thy due than more than all can pay.

22–3. *The service ... itself* Macbeth is just saying 'I was only doing my duty'. Do you think this is a sign of guilt or embarrassment?

24–7. *our duties ... honour* Macbeth's comments indicate an awareness of the value of stable relationships in family and state – relationships which he is soon to shatter brutally.

27. *Safe toward ... honour* with a sure respect to you, in love and honour.

28–9. *I have ... growing* Duncan uses natural imagery to express his spontaneous, warm personality and, in lines 32–3, Banquo's response is in similar terms. Macbeth, on the other hand, is already considering highly unnatural courses.

34. *Wanton* not held back, unlimited.

34–5. *Seek ... sorrow* (my joyful feelings) disguise themselves in tears, which usually express sorrow.

37. *We* Duncan now speaks formally, as king (the royal 'we')

37–9. The throne of Scotland was not hereditary. The king was allowed to appoint his successor from among his relatives (Macbeth was eligible, among others) and usually made him Prince of Cumberland at the same time. This was the recognized title of the heir to the throne, just as Prince of Wales is of the heir to the throne of Great Britain today.

39–42. *which honour ... deservers* My son's new title will not be the only honour to be given out; everyone who deserves recognition will receive it.

42. *From hence to Inverness* Duncan turns to Macbeth, who is to be his host at Inverness.

43. *bind us further to you* Duncan indicates again that he is already deeply in Macbeth's debt for his bravery and success in battle; now he is to be indebted to him as his guest.

44. *The rest ... you;* A rather strained piece of politeness; 'any time or trouble not spent in serving you is hard work'.

45. *harbinger* a man who rode ahead to make arrangements for accommodation for an army or a royal company.

Macbeth
    The service and the loyalty I owe,
    In doing it, pays itself. Your Highness' part
    Is to receive our duties; and our duties
    Are to your throne and state children and servants,   25
    Which do but what they should by doing everything
    Safe toward your love and honour.

Duncan
                         Welcome hither.
    I have begun to plant thee, and will labour
    To make thee full of growing. Noble Banquo,
    That hast no less deserv'd, nor must be known   30
    No less to have done so, let me infold thee
    And hold thee to my heart.

Banquo
                  There if I grow,
    The harvest is your own.

Duncan
                My plenteous joys,
    Wanton in fulness, seek to hide themselves
    In drops of sorrow. Sons, kinsmen, thanes,   35
    And you whose places are the nearest, know
    We will establish our estate upon
    Our eldest, Malcolm, whom we name hereafter
    The Prince of Cumberland; which honour must
    Not unaccompanied invest him only,   40
    But signs of nobleness, like stars, shall shine
    On all deservers. From hence to Inverness,
    And bind us further to you.

Macbeth
    The rest is labour, which is not us'd for you.
    I'll be myself the harbinger, and make joyful   45
    The hearing of my wife with your approach;
    So, humbly take my leave.

Duncan
                My worthy Cawdor!

48–53. Macbeth realises that Duncan making Malcolm the heir to the throne is a serious obstacle if he wishes to be king. So, he commits himself to evil action. His words show he knows only too well how evil his desires are. They are black and deep and fit only for the darkest night.

52–3. *The eye ... to see* Macbeth tries to distance himself from what he is about to do, saying, 'Let my eye be blind to what my hand does, but let the deed be done, even though the murdered body is too horrible to look at.'

54. While Macbeth has been soliloquizing (speaking alone, probably at the front of the stage), Banquo has been praising him to Duncan.

55–6. *And in ... to me* Hearing him praised gives me as much satisfaction as a fine meal eaten with ceremony and in good company.

58. *peerless* unequalled. Some critics have called Duncan a weak king. Is there any evidence for this from what you have read so far?

Macbeth
  [aside] The Prince of Cumberland! That is a step,
  On which I must fall down, or else o'er-leap,
  For in my way it lies. Stars, hide your fires;   50
  Let not light see my black and deep desires.
  The eye wink at the hand; yet let that be
  Which the eye fears, when it is done, to see.

                    [Exit.]

Duncan
  True, worthy Banquo: he is full so valiant;
  And in his commendations I am fed;   55
  It is a banquet to me. Let's after him,
  Whose care is gone before to bid us welcome.
  It is a peerless kinsman.

                [Flourish Exeunt.]

SCENE 5

Macbeth's last words in the previous scene expressed his firm commitment, if horrified, to carry out what needed to be done, and his letter to his wife seems confident. Her reaction to it is one of fierce passion and eagerness. But, she worries that Macbeth's better feelings (human kindness) will stand in the way of ambition, so she plans to overcome them. First she has to cope with the gentler side of her own nature, and does so in a terrible appeal to the forces of evil. When Macbeth finally enters he is guarded in what he says, and does not commit himself one way or the other about the murder.

1. When Lady Macbeth begins to speak she is halfway through the reading of the letter. There is no mention of the witches' promises to Banquo in the part we hear.

2–3. *by the perfects'st report ... knowledge* It sounds as though Macbeth is referring to way the Cawdor prophecy came true.

6. *missives* messengers.

10. *to deliver thee* to pass on to you.

11–12. *the dues of rejoicing* your fair share of joy.

13. *Lay it to thy heart* 'consider well what I have written'. But she probably also takes the words literally by hiding the letter in her bosom.

14–15. *shalt be ... promised* Lady Macbeth begins with a direct statement that her husband shall become king.

17. *To catch the nearest way* to take the shortest route (to what you want).

19. *The illness should attend it* the evil which must go alongside Macbeth's ambition.

19–20. *What thou ... holily* You would like to attain your great ambition without doing anything wrong.

21. *wrongly win* gain what you are not entitled to.

22. *Thou'dst have* You want.

22–3. *that which cries ... have it* the thing (i.e. the crown) which cries 'You must do the murder' if you want it.

24–5. Lady Macbeth knows that Macbeth wishes Duncan to be murdered but that he himself will hesitate to do it.

25. *Hie thee hither* hurry here.

25–30. The crime which Macbeth is considering, has already begun to destroy his character, and is having an equally powerful effect on his wife. All her aggressive, unfeminine instincts are being encouraged, and in lines 40–54 she makes a conscious request that her tender, womanly qualities should be taken away.

Scene 5

Inverness. Macbeth's castle

[Enter LADY MACBETH, *reading a letter.]*

Lady Macbeth
'They met me in the day of success; and I have
learn'd by the perfect'st report they have more in
them than mortal knowledge. When I burn'd in desire
to question them further, they made themselves air,
into which they vanish'd. Whiles I stood rapt in the   5
wonder of it, came missives from the King, who all-
hail'd me "Thane of Cawdor"; by which title, before,
these weird sisters saluted me, and referr'd me to the
coming on of time, with "Hail, king that shalt be!"
This have I thought good to deliver thee, my dearest   10
partner of greatness, that thou mightst not lose the
dues of rejoicing by being ignorant of what greatness
is promis'd thee. Lay it to thy heart, and farewell.'
Glamis thou art, and Cawdor; and shalt be
What thou art promis'd. Yet do I fear thy nature;   15
It is too full o' th' milk of human kindness
To catch the nearest way. Thou wouldst be great;
Art not without ambition, but without
The illness should attend it. What thou wouldst highly
That wouldst thou holily; wouldst not play false,   20
And yet wouldst wrongly win.
Thou'dst have, great Glamis, that which cries
'Thus thou must do' if thou have it;
And that which rather thou dost fear to do
Than wishest should be undone. Hie thee hither,   25
That I may pour my spirits in thine ear,
And chastise with the valour of my tongue

28. *the golden round* the crown.

29. *fate and metaphysical aid* Both powers (fate and the supernatural) are combined in the witches (see note to Act 1, Scene 3, line 33).

31. Lady Macbeth is so astonished by the way fate has placed the king in her hands due to the news that he will shortly arrive that she is taken off her guard.

33. *Would ... preparation* Would have let me know so that I could get things ready.

35. *had the speed of him* was able to ride faster.

36–7. *had scarcely more ... message* gave his news with what was almost his last breath.

37. *Give him tending* Look after him (i.e. get him refreshment, etc.).

38–40. *The raven ... battlements* The raven, an ominous bird, with a harsh croaking cry, is even more hoarse than usual. Lady Macbeth, unlike her husband, does not hesitate for a moment with regard to the crime that is planned. Notice that she says *my battlements*. She has taken over from her husband, in some respects, already.

40–1. *spirits ... thoughts* the spirits which deal with murderous and destructive ideas in human minds.

41. *unsex me here* She appeals to the powers of evil to take away her feminine qualities and to replace them with *direst cruelty.* This is certainly horrible, but note that it implies that she begins by being feminine and having tender feelings. Later, we will find out that she was unable to completely repress her womanly nature (see Act 5, Scene 1). Her tortured sleep-walking suggest she is very much a broken woman, and not an evil monster.

43–4. *Make thick ... remorse* thicken my blood so that pity and sorrow cannot flow through my veins (and soften my heart).

45. *compunctious visitings of nature* pangs of conscience.

46. *fell* deadly.

46–7. *keep peace ... and it* restrain me from putting my purpose into effect.

48. *take my milk for gall* 'change my milk into gall' (an intensely bitter substance).

49. *sightless* invisible.

50. *You wait ... mischief* (wherever) you direct your evil influences in the sphere of nature.

50–4. There is a remarkable similarity between this part of her 'prayer' and Macbeth's *Stars, hide your fires* (Act 1, Scene 4, lines 50–3). However, she welcomes night and darkness with much more

All that Impedes thee from the golden round
Which fate and metaphysical aid doth seem
To have thee crown'd withal.

[Enter a MESSENGER.*]*

What is your tidings?   30
Messenger
  The King comes here to-night.
Lady Macbeth
                    Thou'rt mad to say it.
  Is not thy master with him? who, were't so,
  Would have inform'd for preparation.
Messenger
  So please you, it is true. Our Thane is coming.
  One of my fellows had the speed of him,   35
  Who, almost dead for breath, had scarcely more
  Than would make up his message.
Lady Macbeth
                    Give him tending:
  He brings great news.

[Exit MESSENGER.*]*

            The raven himself is hoarse
  That croaks the fatal entrance of Duncan
  Under my battlements. Come, you spirits   40
  That tend on mortal thoughts, unsex me here;
  And fill me, from the crown to the toe, top-full
  Of direst cruelty. Make thick my blood,
  Stop up th' access and passage to remorse,
  That no compunctious visitings of nature   45
  Shake my fell purpose nor keep peace between
  Th' effect and it. Come to my woman's breasts,
  And take my milk for gall, you murd'ring ministers,
  Wherever in your sightless substances
  You wait on nature's mischief. Come, thick night,   50

determination than her husband. In her attempt to block out Heaven, note that she again uses the word *my*; this time it is *my keen knife*, as though she intends to commit the murder herself.

51. *pall thee* shroud yourself.

51. *dunnest* darkest.

54. *Hold* Stop.

55. *the all-hail hereafter* these words are very close to those of the Third Witch's

57. *This ignorant present* the present which knows nothing of the future.

57–8. *I feel now ... instant* She stresses that the deed is as good as done, the crown virtually gained already. Macbeth does not respond to this, although he must understand it. Note the contrast between Lady Macbeth's eager confidence and Macbeth's reluctance.

60–1. *O, never Shall ... morrow see* She says emphatically that the next morning will not *see* Duncan departing. There is also a hint of god-like power about the words, as though she and Macbeth between them could stop the sun rising. Ross's account of the wild weather of the following morning (Act 2, Scene 4, lines 5–10) shows that there is something unintentionally prophetic in her words.

63. *beguile the time* 'deceive everyone' (i.e. those present on the occasion).

64. *Look like the time* put on an expression which suits the occasion.

66–8. These dreadful euphemisms (phrases that hide the reality) such as ***provided for*** and ***This night's great business*** may be signs that Lady Macbeth is not as ruthless as she would wish.

68. *into my dispatch* 'Leave it all to me' she says, but she also puns on the word *dispatch*, which means both 'management' and 'killing'.

69–70. (Tonight's events) will give us absolute power for the rest of our lives.

71. Macbeth does not share her confidence in the outcome, and cannot look her in the eye, as her next remark shows.

72. To change one's expression always reveals fear (and suspicion is aroused).

And pall thee in the dunnest smoke of hell
That my keen knife see not the wound it makes,
Nor heaven peep through the blanket of the dark
To cry 'Hold, hold'.

[Enter MACBETH.*]*

      Great Glamis! Worthy Cawdor!
Greater than both, by the all-hail hereafter!   55
Thy letters have transported me beyond
This ignorant present, and I feel now
The future in the instant.
Macbeth
      My dearest love,
Duncan comes here to-night.
Lady Macbeth
      And when goes hence?
Macbeth
To-morrow – as he purposes.
Lady Macbeth
      O, never   60
Shall sun that morrow see!
Your face, my thane, is as a book where men
May read strange matters. To beguile the time,
Look like the time; bear welcome in your eye,
Your hand, your tongue; look like th' innocent
   flower,   65
But be the serpent under't. He that's coming
Must be provided for; and you shall put
This night's great business into my dispatch;
Which shall to all our nights and days to come
Give solely sovereign sway and masterdom.   70
Macbeth
We will speak further.
Lady Macbeth
      Only look up clear.
To alter favour ever is to fear.
Leave all the rest to me.

[Exeunt.]

35

SCENE 6

There is a dreadful irony about this scene, with the innocent king delighting in the appearance of the Macbeths' castle. He also comments on the generous hospitality of the Macbeths themselves. Lady Macbeth seems almost to overdo her humble greeting (lines 14–20) but the king suspects nothing. Do you see him as naive or even senile in his innocence?

Stage Direction *Hautboys* oboes.

1. *seat* situation.
3. *gentle senses* Perhaps Duncan means that his senses have become less acute with age; in any case the word helps to build up our impression of him.
3. *guest of summer* migrant bird
4. *martlet* This is almost certainly the house-martin, and not the swift (which is its modern meaning). Banquo suggests that it prefers to build its nest on church walls (again, very ironic, given what is about to happen!)
4. *approve* show.
5. *By his lov'd mansionry* by the fact that it chooses the castle for its home-building.
5–6. *the heaven's breath ... here* the breezes are soft and attractive here.
6. *jutty* projecting part of the building.
8. *pendent bed and procreant cradle* the hanging nests in which the birds produce their young.
10. *delicate* soft and sweet.
11–14. Duncan seems to be saying something like this: 'I am sometimes bothered by the love my attendants show me (perhaps because he is such a modest man) but I always acknowledge it. You should pray God to reward me for the trouble I am causing you'.

14–20. Lady Macbeth returns Duncan's compliment in perfect politeness. We know she is insincere, but we also recognize her skill here. Briefly, she is saying that, even if her efforts were quadrupled, they would not measure up to the honour of having the king as a visitor.

20. *We rest your hermits* 'We will always pray for you' (like a religious recluse).

Scene 6

Inverness. Before Macbeth's castle

[Hautboys and torches. Enter DUNCAN, MALCOLM,
DONALBAIN, BANQUO, LENNOX, MACDUFF, ROSS, ANGUS
and ATTENDANTS.*]*

Duncan
    This castle hath a pleasant seat; the air
    Nimbly and sweetly recommends itself
    Unto our gentle senses.
Banquo
                  This guest of summer,
    The temple-haunting martlet, does approve
    By his lov'd mansionry that the heaven's breath   5
    Smells wooingly here; no jutty, frieze,
    Buttress, nor coign of vantage, but this bird
    Hath made her pendent bed and procreant cradle.
    Where they most breed and haunt, I have observed
    The air is delicate.

[Enter LADY MACBETH.*]*

Duncan
              See, see, our honour'd hostess!   10
    The love that follows us sometime is our trouble,
    Which still we thank as love. Herein I teach you
    How you shall bid God 'ield us for your pains,
    And thank us for your trouble.
Lady Macbeth
                   All our service
    In every point twice done, and then done double,   15
    Were poor and single business to contend
    Against those honours deep and broad wherewith
    Your Majesty loads our house; for those of old,
    And the late dignities heap'd up to them,
    We rest your hermits.

22. *purveyor* one who went on ahead of a king to prepare accommodation for him.
23. *holp* helped.

25–8. Your servants always have their servants, themselves and everything that belongs to them ready to please your Highness, and to offer to him what is really his already.

31. *By your leave* He is really repeating that he wants to take her hand, or else he kisses her on the cheek.

Duncan
                              Where's the Thane of Cawdor?   20
    We cours'd him at the heels and had a purpose
    To be his purveyor; but he rides well,
    And his great love, sharp as his spur, hath holp him
    To his home before us. Fair and noble hostess,
    We are your guest to-night.
Lady Macbeth
                              Your servants ever   25
    Have theirs, themselves, and what is theirs, in compt,
    To make their audit at your Highness' pleasure,
    Still to return your own.
Duncan
                          Give me your hand;
    Conduct me to mine host. We love him highly,
    And shall continue our graces towards him.   30
    By your leave, hostess.

                    [Exeunt.]

SCENE 7

In this scene Macbeth argues a convincing case against murdering Duncan, and decides against it. However, the force of Lady Macbeth's scorn and eloquence changes his mind; her determination and confidence brush aside his fears and scruples.

Stage Direction *Sewer* This word originally meant the servant who tasted the food of a prominent person to make sure that it was not poisoned. Here it seems to refer to the man who superintends the laying of the banquet table.

1–28. This speech, like most Shakespeare soliloquies, provides an opportunity for the speaker to reveal how he really feels. In this case, Macbeth begins uneasily arguing with himself, perhaps almost muttering, but later he becomes deeply moved and eloquent.

1. The first *done* means 'over and done with'.

2–3. *If th'assassination ... consequence* if the murder could be completely decisive and without unpleasant results.

3. *trammel* entangle in a net

4. *surcease* death.

5. *here* on earth.

6. *this bank and shoal of time* Macbeth seems to view human life as a sandbank in eternity, as if he were in a shipwreck, stuck and unable to go forward or back.

7. *We'd jump the life to come* I'd risk what comes after death.

8–10. Macbeth is worried that a bloody act often provokes bloody retaliation.

10–12. *This even-handed justice ... lips:* Justice rules that we should drink the poison we give to others.

12–28. Macbeth now speaks with real emotion, and in doing so reveals a genuine respect for Duncan's goodness, and also a respect for decent human values. He fully understands how evil the act of murder is.

12–16. The *double trust* is that he is both a relative and a subject of the king, and is also the king's host!

17. *Hath borne ... meek* Has used his authority as king with such genuine humility.

18. *clear* innocent.

20. *taking-off* murder.

21–5. Cherubs were not chubby babies (as we think of them today) but senior angels. But both baby and angels are riding the winds *(blast* and *sightless couriers or* invisible runners) and they are all, in Macbeth's vivid imagination, going to make the crime known everyone *(blow the horrid deed in every eye).*

Scene 7

Inverness. Macbeth's castle

[Hautboys, torches. Enter a SEWER, *and divers* SERVANTS
with dishes and service over the stage. Then enter
MACBETH.*]*

Macbeth
 If it were done when 'tis done, then 'twere well
 It were done quickly. If th' assassination
 Could trammel up the consequence, and catch,
 With his surcease, success; that but this blow
 Might be the be-all and the end-all here –   5
 But here upon this bank and shoal of time –
 We'd jump the life to come. But in these cases
 We still have judgment here, that we but teach
 Bloody instructions, which being taught return
 To plague th' inventor. This even-handed justice 10
 Commends th' ingredience of our poison'd chalice
 To our own lips. He's here in double trust:
 First, as I am his kinsman and his subject –
 Strong both against the deed; then, as his host,
 Who should against his murderer shut the door, 15
 Not bear the knife myself. Besides, this Duncan
 Hath borne his faculties so meek, hath been
 So clear in his great office, that his virtues
 Will plead like angels, trumpet-tongu'd, against
 The deep damnation of his taking-off;   20
 And pity, like a naked new-born babe,
 Striding the blast, or heaven's cherubin hors'd
 Upon the sightless couriers of the air,
 Shall blow the horrid deed in every eye,
 That tears shall drown the wind. I have no spur 25
 To prick the sides of my intent, but only

27–8. Jumping directly into one's saddle was a young man's way of showing-off. Possibly Shakespeare means 'overshoots and falls to the ground on the other side' by the last few words. Or it could mean simply that the rider, having cleared an obstacle, falls off his horse on the other side of it.

29. This is the first of several occasions when Lady Macbeth sharply questions her husband on his actions.

31. Macbeth's statement sounds decisive, and it certainly follows on logically from his recent argument with himself, but it does not take Lady Macbeth very long to make him retreat.

32–5. It is interesting that Macbeth does not mention to his wife the objections to the murder that appear to carry most weight with him – the moral and ethical objections. To her he merely talks about ruining his reputation *(Golden opinions)*.

34. *in their newest gloss* like fresh, new clothes, perfectly clean.

35–7. Lady Macbeth takes up Macbeth's metaphor from clothing and mixes it with one from drunkenness. She goes on to suggest that Macbeth is like someone waking up with a hangover *(green and pale)* who forgets or ignores what he had decided to do when he was drunk.

39–41. *Art thou afeard ... in desire ?* Are you afraid to put firmly into practice what you really want to do?

39–45. She uses two very powerful (and unfair) weapons here. She says 'I see you don't really love me' *(From this time Such I account thy love)* and accuses him of being a coward. Macbeth has no defence against such tactics.

45. *th' adage* the proverb. Lady Macbeth is referring to 'The cat who would like to catch fish, but isn't prepared to get her feet wet...'. The ridiculousness of the comparison between Macbeth and the cat seems to affect him deeply because he asks her to be quiet.

47–8. *What beast was't then ... to me?* Does this reference to an *enterprise* that Macbeth has discussed with his wife suggest that they have talked about the murder 'off-stage', i.e. in a scene that Shakespeare has not written for us? Or was Macbeth't letter to his wife a clear enough reference to the plan?

Vaulting ambition, which o'er-leaps itself,
And falls on th' other.

[Enter LADY MACBETH.]

                    How now! What news?
Lady Macbeth
   He has almost supp'd. Why have you left the chamber?
Macbeth
   Hath he ask'd for me?
Lady Macbeth
               Know you not he has?   30
Macbeth
   We will proceed no further in this business.
   He hath honour'd me of late; and I have bought
   Golden opinions from all sorts of people,
   Which would be worn now in their newest gloss,
   Not cast aside so soon.
Lady Macbeth
                Was the hope drunk   35
   Wherein you dress'd yourself? Hath it slept since,
   And wakes it now to look so green and pale
   At what it did so freely? From this time
   Such I account thy love. Art thou afeard
   To be the same in thine own act and valour   40
   As thou art in desire? Wouldst thou have that
   Which thou esteem'st the ornament of life,
   And live a coward in thine own esteem,
   Letting 'I dare not' wait upon 'I would',
   Like the poor cat i' th' adage?
Macbeth
                  Prithee, peace;   45
   I dare do all that may become a man;
   Who dares do more is none.
Lady Macbeth
                What beast was't then
   That made you break this enterprise to me?

50–1. *And to be more ... the man* You would be even more brave and manly if you made yourself king, rather than just a thane.

51–4. *Nor ... you* When there was no opportunity, you wished to create one; now when the opportunity presents itself, you are afraid to take it.

54–9. Lady Macbeth has seen the effect of her taunts on her husband and now comes out with the most outrageous and shocking statement of all. It sounds as though the ***murd'ring ministers*** she appealed to (Act 1, Scene 5, lines 47–8) have done as she asked; yet the force of these words depends on her and her husband's awareness that they are horrible and unnatural. In reply all Macbeth can say is, feebly, ***If we should fail?***

60. *We fail!* How do you think she says these words – realistically ('Well, then, we fail') or scornfully ('How could we possibly fail?')?

64. *chamberlains* officials of the royal bedchamber.

65. *wine and wassail* drink and partying. It almost sounds as though Lady Macbeth intends personally to spend time with them, urging them to enjoy themselves, but probably she proposes simply to leave them plenty of drink, and encourage them to have a good time after she has left.

66–8. *That memory ... only* Memory, the keeper of one part of the brain, will be turned into smoke by the drink, which will smother the rest of the brain, where the rational part is.

68. *limbec* alembic, a kind of retort.

69. *drenched* drowned – but a 'drench' is animal medicine (e.g. poured down a horse's throat from a bottle) so perhaps this hints at the way Lady Macbeth views these puppets in her dreadful game – as animals?

72. *spongy* drunken.

73. *quell* murder (the word comes from the same origin as 'kill').

74. *mettle* spirit, temperament.

75. *receiv'd* accepted.

When you durst do it, then you were a man;
And to be more than what you were, you would   50
Be so much more the man. Nor time nor place
Did then adhere, and yet you would make both;
They have made themselves, and that their fitness now
Does unmake you. I have given suck, and know
How tender 'tis to love the babe that milks me –   55
I would, while it was smiling in my face,
Have pluck'd my nipple from his boneless gums,
And dash'd the brains out, had I so sworn
As you have done to this.

Macbeth

                     If we should fail?

Lady Macbeth

    We fail!   60
But screw your courage to the sticking place,
And we'll not fail. When Duncan is asleep –
Whereto the rather shall his day's hard journey
Soundly invite him – his two chamberlains
Will I with wine and wassail so convince   65
That memory, the warder of the brain,
Shall be a fume, and the receipt of reason
A limbec only. When in swinish sleep
Their drenched natures lie as in a death,
What cannot you and I perform upon   70
Th' unguarded Duncan? what not put upon
His spongy officers, who shall bear the guilt
Of our great quell?

Macbeth

                Bring forth men-children only;
For thy undaunted mettle should compose
Nothing but males. Will it not be receiv'd,   75
When we have mark'd with blood those sleepy two
Of his own chamber, and us'd their very daggers,
That they have done't?

80. *bend up* i.e. like a man preparing a crossbow for firing.

81. *Each corporal agent* All my physical powers.

82–3. Although now *settled,* Macbeth remains fully aware of the deceit and wickedness involved, whereas, at times, his wife seems to be able to delude herself that there is glory in the deed (e.g. line 73, *great quell*. Macbeth calls it a *deep damnation* in line 20, and a *terrible feat* in line 81).

Lady Macbeth
                  Who dares receive it other,
As we shall make our griefs and clamour roar
Upon his death?
Macbeth
                I am settled, and bend up   80
Each corporal agent to this terrible feat.
Away, and mock the time with fairest show;
False face must hide what the false heart doth know.

      [Exeunt.]

ACT 2 SCENE 1

Apart from developing the story, and creating the atmosphere of
horror before the murder, this scene also shows the difference
between Banquo and Macbeth. Banquo and his son Fleance are good
companions, and Banquo, suffering from *cursed thoughts,* appeals
to the *Merciful powers of* goodness for help in fighting them. He also
makes it fairly clear just afterwards that he is not happy about
Macbeth's association with the witches.

1–5. As usual in the daylight of the Elizabethan theatre, it is
necessary for Shakespeare to convey the time of day with words.

4. *There's husbandry in heaven* 'They are being thrifty up in
heaven' (they have put their candles – stars – out).
5. *that* Having given Fleance his sword Banquo probably hands him
his shield or cloak or dagger. Then, when Macbeth enters (line 9) his
first instinct is to ask for his sword back, quickly.
6. *A heavy summons* i.e. to sleep.

13. *unusual pleasure* Probably because he is so appreciative of
Macbeth's recent services and so confident of his thane's support and
loyalty.
14. *largess* generous gifts.
14. *offices* servants' quarters.
15. *withal* with.
16–17. *shut up In measureless content* Duncan's day has ended in
unlimited happiness.

ACT 2
Scene 1

Inverness. Court of Macbeth's castle

[Enter BANQUO, *and* FLEANCE *with a torch before him.]*

Banquo
How goes the night, boy?
Fleance
The moon is down; I have not heard the clock.
Banquo
And she goes down at twelve.
Fleance

                  I tak't, 'tis later, sir.

Banquo
Hold, take my sword. There's husbandry in heaven;
Their candles are all out. Take thee that too.   5
A heavy summons lies like lead upon me,
And yet I would not sleep. Merciful powers
Restrain in me the cursed thoughts that nature
Gives way to in repose!

    [Enter MACBETH *and a* SERVANT *with a torch.]*

                Give me my sword.
Who's there?   10
Macbeth
A friend.
Banquo
What, sir, not yet at rest? The king's a-bed.
He hath been in unusual pleasure, and
Sent forth great largess to your offices.
This diamond he greets your wife withal,   15
By the name of most kind hostess; and shut up
In measureless content.

49

17–19. *Being unprepar'd ... have wrought* Because we were not prepared, our wish to provide the king with generous hospitality could not be fulfilled.

22–4. *Yet, when ... the time* When we can find a convenient time, let us talk about the witches – if you are willing to do so.

25–6. These words of Macbeth's are deliberately vague. They could mean 'If you will follow my advice at the appropriate time' or 'If you will join my group of supporters *(consent)* when we emerge'.

26–29. Banquo's reply, refusing to commit himself to anyone, could be seen as equally unclear, and mean that either he is waiting to see what lies in store for him (after all, the witches have said his heirs will be king) or that he is rejecting the path Macbeth wishes to take. Either way, it is clear to Macbeth that Banquo is suspicious of him, and that he can't count on him for absolute support.

27. *augment* increase.

28. *bosom franchis'd and allegiance clear* my conscience free from guilt and my allegiance innocent.

29. *I shall be counselled* I will accept your advice.

33–49. In the first part of this soliloquy Macbeth is revealed even more deeply than usual in such speeches, for the illusion of the bloody dagger shows us what we would now call his subconscious mind. Like Lady Macbeth he is denying his own true nature in preparing to commit the murder, and one of the penalties is a *heat-oppressed brain.*

Macbeth
                          Being unprepar'd,
  Our will became the servant to defect;
  Which else should free have wrought.

Banquo
                                   All's well.
  I dreamt last night of the three Weird Sisters,   20
  To you they have show'd some truth.

Macbeth
                          I think not of them;
  Yet, when we can entreat an hour to serve,
  We would spend it in some words upon that business,
  If you would grant the time.

Banquo
                        At your kind'st leisure.

Macbeth
  If you shall cleave to my consent, when 'tis,   25
  It shall make honour for you.

Banquo
                         So I lose none
  In seeking to augment it, but still keep
  My bosom franchis'd and allegiance clear,
  I shall be counsell'd.

Macbeth
                    Good repose the while!

Banquo
  Thanks, air; the like to you!   30

        [Exeunt BANQUO *and* FLEANCE.*]*

Macbeth
  Go bid thy mistress, when my drink is ready,
  She strike upon the bell. Get thee to bed.

             [Exit SERVANT.*]*

  Is this a dagger which I see before me,
  The handle toward my hand? Come, let me clutch thee.

36–7. *sensible To feeling as to sight?* (something that can be) touched as well as seen?

39. *heat-oppressed* feverish.
40. *palpable* touchable.

42. The dagger is probably moving towards Duncan's bedroom, as though it is encouraging Macbeth to go and do the deed.

44–5. *Mine eyes ... the rest* Either my eyes are deceived (my other senses tell me there is no dagger) or else they are worth all my other senses put together (what I see really is a dagger).

46. *dudgeon* handle.
46. *gouts* drops.
48. *the bloody business* the murder plan playing on his imagination.
49. *the one half-world* the darkened northern hemisphere.
51. *curtain'd sleep* sleep behind closed eyelids, or behind the curtains of a four-poster bed.
52. *Pale Hecate's offerings* The goddess of witchcraft's rituals.
52–6. *and wither'd murder...* Murder, personified as an aged, perhaps skeleton-like man, is awakened by the howl of a wolf, which keeps the time for him, and he moves stealthily, ghost-like (or in the same way that Tarquin went to rape Lucretia), to do his killing. Tarquin was an infamous King of Ancient Rome who raped the very virtuous Lucretia.
58. *prate* talk.
60. *threat* threaten.
61. He is telling himself to stop talking and get on with it.
62. The sound of the bell comes before the murder; the sound of knocking on the gate follows it.

63. *knell* a funeral bell

I have thee not, and yet I see thee still.   35
Art thou not, fatal vision, sensible
To feeling as to sight? or art thou but
A dagger of the mind, a false creation,
Proceeding from the heat-oppressed brain?
I see thee yet, in form as palpable   40
As this which now I draw.
Thou marshall'st me the way that I was going;
And such an instrument I was to use.
Mine eyes are made the fools o' th' other senses,
Or else worth all the rest. I see thee still;   45
And on thy blade and dudgeon gouts of blood,
Which was not so before. There's no such thing:
It is the bloody business which informs
Thus to mine eyes. Now o'er the one half-world
Nature seems dead, and wicked dreams abuse   50
The curtain'd sleep; now witchcraft celebrates
Pale Hecate's offerings; and wither'd murder,
Alarum'd by his sentinel the wolf,
Whose howl's his watch, thus with his stealthy pace,
With Tarquin's ravishing strides, towards his design   55
Moves like a ghost. Thou sure and firm-set earth,
Hear not my steps which way they walk, for fear
Thy very stones prate of my whereabout
And take the present horror from the time,
Which now suits with it. Whiles I threat, he lives;   60
Words to the heat of deeds too cold breath gives.

                    [A bell rings.]

I go, and it is done; the bell invites me.
Hear it not, Duncan, for it is a knell
That summons thee to heaven or to hell.

                    [Exit.]

                         53

SCENE 2

Lady Macbeth now reveals that she, too, like the chamberlains she mentioned earlier, has been drinking, but in her case the effect has been to give her an artificial courage. Is this perhaps another sign that she is not quite as tough as she seems?

2. *quench'd* put them out (like extinguished candles); in contrast, Lady Macbeth has been 'set alight' by the drink.

2. *Hark!* in spite of everything she is still capable of being frightened, in this case by an owl's cry.

3. The cry of an owl was thought to indicate that someone was about to die.

3–4. *the fatal bellman ... good-night* the night before a man was to be executed an official used to ring a bell outside the door of his cell.

4. *stern'st good-night* the final, most serious farewell, when a man is about to die.

4. *He is about it* Macbeth is now murdering the king.

5. *surfeited* having had too much of something, in this case strong drink. The word *groom* was applied to any low-grade servant. These grooms are attendants on the king who act as bodyguards.

6. *mock their charge with snores* they show how hopelessly they have failed by snoring while on duty.

6. *drugg'd their possets* a posset was a nightcap containing milk, egg and some alcoholic drink, with other ingredients. Lady Macbeth had made quite sure that the men would be put out of action by adding a drug to the drink.

7. *nature* life. Life and death are here thought of as two persons each of whom argues that the grooms belong to him.

8. Like his wife, Macbeth is startled by a sound. The effect of his frightened shout is all the greater because it comes from off-stage.

10–11. *Th' attempt ... Confounds us* if, as I fear, he has tried to kill the king but failed, we shall be ruined.

11. *I laid their daggers ready* Lady Macbeth has taken the grooms' daggers out of their scabbards and left them ready for Macbeth to do the stabbing. In his absent-minded horror Macbeth comes in with these daggers. How do you think he is carrying them?

13. *My husband!* what emotions do you think are packed into these words? Surprise? Admiration? Any others?

15. Both owls and crickets were thought to foretell death.

Scene 2

Inverness. Macbeth's castle

[Enter LADY MACBETH.*]*

Lady Macbeth
  That which hath made them drunk hath made me bold
  What hath quench'd them hath given me fire.
     Hark! Peace!
  It was the owl that shriek'd, the fatal bellman,
  Which gives the stern'st good-night. He is about it.
  The doors are open; and the surfeited grooms   5
  Do mock their charge with snores. I have drugg'd
     their possets,
  That death and nature do contend about them,
  Whether they live or die.
Macbeth
  [within]   Who's there! What, ho!
Lady Macbeth
  Alack! I am afraid they have awak'd,
  And 'tis not done. Th' attempt, and not the deed,   10
  Confounds us. Hark! I laid their daggers ready;
  He could not miss 'em. Had he not resembled
  My father as he slept, I had done't.

[Enter MACBETH.*]*

                  My husband!
Macbeth
  I have done the deed. Didst thou not hear a noise?
Lady Macbeth
  I heard the owl scream and the crickets cry.   15
  Did not you speak?
Macbeth
         When?
Lady Macbeth
         Now.

16–20. The jerky conversation obviously adds to the tension in the audience and also shows how jumpy Macbeth and his wife are.

19. Why does Lady Macbeth mention only Donalbain, when Malcolm too seems to be sleeping in the *second chamber* (next room)?

20. *sorry* wretched, miserable.

22. Who are these two men? It's not absolutely clear, but it is perhaps more likely they are the king's sons rather than the grooms, given that they say 'their prayers'.

25. *There are two lodg'd together* Lady Macbeth is pointing out that, as the two princes – if it is them – are sharing a room, the disturbance may be confined to them.

27. *hangman's hands* the word *hangman* was used for an executioner, whatever method he used; but since he usually 'drew' and 'quartered' the body (disembowelled it and cut it into pieces) even when the man had been hanged, a hangman's hands would often have been covered with blood.

28. *List'ning their fear* listening to

35–9. In this speech Macbeth expresses his horror at the fact that he has killed a man in the helpless innocence of sleep; in his imagination he condemns himself to a fitting punishment – never to sleep again.

Macbeth

As I descended?

Lady Macbeth
   Ay.

Macbeth
   Hark!
   Who lies i' th' second chamber?

Lady Macbeth

Donalbain.

Macbeth
   [looking on his hands] This is a sorry sight.   20

Lady Macbeth
   A foolish thought to say a sorry sight.

Macbeth
   There's one did laugh in's sleep, and one cried 'Murder!'
   That they did wake each other. I stood and heard them
   But they did say their prayers, and address'd them
   Again to sleep.

Lady Macbeth

There are two lodg'd together.   25

Macbeth
   One cried 'God bless us,' and 'Amen' the other,
   As they had seen me with these hangman's hands.
   List'ning their fear, I could not say 'Amen'
   When they did say 'God bless us!'

Lady Macbeth

Consider it not so deeply.   30

Macbeth
   But wherefore could not I pronounce 'Amen'?
   I had most need of blessing, and 'Amen'
   Stuck in my throat.

Lady Macbeth

These deeds must not be thought
   After these ways: so, it will make us mad.

Macbeth
   Methought I heard a voice cry 'Sleep no more;   35
   Macbeth does murder sleep' – the innocent sleep,

37. *knits up the ravell'd sleave* probably *sleave* means a piece of coarse silk; it has become (as we say) unravelled or frayed, but can be restored by knitting or stitching. In modern terms, sleep helps to soothe frayed nerves.

38. *sore labour's bath* like a refreshing bath after a hard day's work

39–40. *great nature's second course. Chief nourisher in life's feast* a pudding or sweet used to be the first course at dinner; the main meat dish came after it.

44. Lady Macbeth, always more practical than her husband, is puzzled to know who could have been making the frightening comments about sleep.

45–6. She shows a familiar reaction to evidence of his mental instability; 'Pull yourself together and don't be silly (brainsick)!'

46. *Go get some water* … an apparently sensible, realistic way of dealing with the situation, but later it will prove completely inadequate as she tries to rid herself of the memory of the crime. (See Act 5, Scene 1, line 40: *What, will these hands ne'er be clean?*)

47. *witness* evidence.

52. *Infirm of purpose!* Lady Macbeth's most effective way of bullying her husband is to comment scornfully on his weak will.

53–5. *The sleeping* … she sounds strong and confident now, in contrast with Macbeth, yet earlier in this very scene (lines 12–13) she saw Duncan with *the eye of childhood* herself, and could not kill him.

55. *A painted devil* a mere picture of a devil.

56–7. *gild the faces* paint with blood. Her use of the word *guilt* is a pun on 'gilt', a layer of gold (although of course here the layer will be red). Do you find such punning out of place at such a terrible moment? For the Elizabethans they often conveyed tension and irony, not just rather obvious humour.

57. *Whence is that knocking?* Macbeth takes the knocking at first to be a supernatural thing. In the next scene we find out that Macduff and Lennox have been knocking at the castle gate in order to come in and wake the king.

59. Macbeth is becoming so obsessed with the sight of his own bloody hands that they almost blind him.

60. Neptune was the Roman god of the sea.

Sleep that knits up the ravell'd sleave of care,
The death of each day's life, sore labour's bath,
Balm of hurt minds, great nature's second course,
Chief nourisher in life's feast.

Lady Macbeth

What do you mean?   40

Macbeth

Still it cried 'Sleep no more' to all the house;
'Glamis hath murder'd sleep; and therefore Cawdor
Shall sleep no more – Macbeth shall sleep no more'.

Lady Macbeth

Who was it that thus cried? Why, worthy Thane,
You do unbend your noble strength to think   45
So brainsickly of things. Go get some water
And wash this filthy witness from your hand.
Why did you bring these daggers from the place?
They must lie there. Go carry them, and smear
The sleepy grooms with blood.

Macbeth

I'll go no more: 50
I am afraid to think what I have done;
Look on't again I dare not.

Lady Macbeth

Infirm of purpose!
Give me the daggers. The sleeping and the dead
Are but as pictures; 'tis the eye of childhood
That fears a painted devil. If he do bleed,   55
I'll gild the faces of the grooms withal,
For it must seem their guilt.

[Exit. Knocking within.]

Macbeth

Whence is that knocking?
How is't with me, when every noise appals me?
What hands are here? Ha! they pluck out mine eyes.
Will all great Neptune's ocean wash this blood   60

61–3. Macbeth says that if he tries to wash his hands in the sea there is so much blood it will make the whole ocean red.

62. *multitudinous* vast.

62. *incarnadine* turn red (literally flesh-coloured). After putting this wildly imaginative idea in long words derived from Latin, Shakespeare almost repeats it in short Anglo-Saxon words.

63. *one red* entirely red.

65. *a heart so white* accusations of cowardice are another of Lady Macbeth's weapons against her husband.

67. She sounds confident but she too is later obsessed with the impossibility of washing the blood away (Act 5, Scene 1).

70. They have not changed into their night-clothes so far. She reminds him to do so, otherwise those who are knocking will think it strange that she and Macbeth are up and about, fully-clothed, in the middle of the night.

73. Macbeth knows that he cannot face fully the deed he has done, and take responsibility for it.

Clean from my hand? No; this my hand will rather
The multitudinous seas incarnadine,
Making the green one red.

[Re-enter LADY MACBETH.*]*

Lady Macbeth
    My hands are of your colour; but I shame
    To wear a heart so white. *[Knock]* I hear a knocking   65
    At the south entry; retire we to our chamber.
    A little water clears us of this deed.
    How easy is it then! Your constancy
    Hath left you unattended. *[Knock]* Hark! more knocking,
    Get on your nightgown, lest occasion call us   70
    And show us to be watchers. Be not lost
    So poorly in your thoughts.
Macbeth
    To know my deed, 'twere best not know myself. *[Knock]*
    Wake Duncan with thy knocking! I would thou couldst!

[Exeunt.]

SCENE 3

It may seem strange that the Porter's speech and conversation with Macduff and Lennox comes here, and some critics have even claimed that Shakespeare didn't write this opening. However, the audience do need *some* relief after the tension of the previous scene; it is certainly ironically appropriate that the Porter compares himself with the *porter of hell-gate,* and this is almost what he is given what has just happened. The unlocking of the gate also brings in the decent, outside world and introduces us to the central figure of Macduff.

2. The word *old* was often used in the sense of much, a lot of.

4. *Beelzebub* Satan's lieutenant – but the name is often used of the Devil himself.

4–5. *Here's a farmer ... plenty* The Porter imagines himself to be a kind of guide showing us round Hell. The first of the damned he sees is a farmer who has committed suicide because the good harvest will put the price of corn down.

5–6. *Come in time ... sweat for't* Come early, then you can enjoy the bonfire of Hell and sweat freely, so you'll need cloths to wipe yourself.

7. *i' th' other devil's name?* It sounds as though the Porter cannot remember the name of any other devil.

8. *equivocator* Probably a Jesuit priest, because the Jesuits were then believed to use words deceptively (to equivocate) in their defence against charges of treason.

9. *the scales* Justice, personified as a woman, held scales in which to balance the evidence.

10–11. *could not equivocate to heaven* A well-known Jesuit called Garnet was hanged and that ended all his equivocation ... perhaps Shakespeare is referring to him.

12–13. *an English tailor ... French hose* Tailors had a reputation for making clothes their customers ordered with the minimum of material and keeping the rest themselves. French hose had been very full and loose, and this gave the thieving tailors plenty of scope. But the French fashion had recently changed and tight hose made it obvious when they got up to their cloth-stealing tricks.

14. *roast your goose* A goose was a tailor's smoothing-iron, but the phrase probably also meant something like 'kill the goose that laid the golden eggs', i.e. the tailor has tried his trick once too often and will profit no more from stealing customers' material.

18. *the primrose way ... bonfire* the pleasant, easy path to Hell.

19–20. *remember the porter* He is suggesting that they should tip him (even though he has taken so long to open the gate).

Scene 3

Inverness. Macbeth's castle

[Knocking within. Enter a PORTER.]

Porter

Here's a knocking indeed! If a man were porter of
hell-gate, he should have old turning the key. *[Knock]*
Knock, knock, knock! Who's there, i' th' name of
Beelzebub? Here's a farmer that hang'd himself on
th' expectation of plenty. Come in time; have napkins   5
enow about you; here you'll sweat for't. *[Knock]*
Knock, knock! Who's there, i' th' other devil's name?
Faith, here's an equivocator, that could swear in both
the scales against either scale; who committed treason
enough for God's sake, yet could not equivocate to   10
heaven. O, come in, equivocator. *[Knock]* Knock,
knock! Who's there? Faith, here's an English tailor
come hither for stealing out of a French hose. Come
in, tailor, here you may roast your goose. *[Knock]*
Knock, knock; never at quiet! What are you? But this   15
place is too cold for hell. I'll devil-porter it no further.
I had thought to have let in some of all professions
that go the primrose way to th' everlasting bonfire.
[Knock] Anon, anon! *[Opens the gate]* I pray you
remember the porter.   20

[Enter MACDUFF and LENNOX.]

Macduff

Was it so late, friend, ere you went to bed, that you
do lie so late?

23. *carousing* drinking riotously.

23. *second cock* This was a way of saying 'three o'clock in the morning'.

23–40. In this conversation the Porter plays the part of a typical Elizabethan working-man as shown on stage, making rude jokes and relishing playing with words, while Macduff is the upper-class listener, willing to go along with the joke for a while.

26. *nose-painting* getting yourself a red nose (from too much alcohol)

Lechery lust.

29. *equivocator* deceiver.

33. *equivocates him in a sleep* sends him to sleep and gives him lustful dreams (but no satisfaction for his lust).

33–4 & 35. *giving him the lie ... gave thee the lie* These could mean 'to lay out', as in wrestling or boxing.

36–9. The Porter plays with the wrestling metaphor and the idea of relieving himself.

36. *requited him* paid him back.

38–9. *made a shift* managed.

42. *Good morrow* Good morning.

44. *timely* early.

Porter

  Faith, sir, we were carousing till the second cock; and
  drink, sir, is a great provoker of three things.

Macduff

  What three things does drink especially provoke?   25

Porter

  Marry, sir, nose-painting, sleep, and urine. Lechery,
  sir, it provokes and unprovokes; it provokes the
  desire, but it takes away the performance. Therefore
  much drink may be said to be an equivocator with
  lechery: it makes him, and it mars him; it sets him on,   30
  and it takes him off; it persuades him, and disheartens
  him; makes him stand to, and not stand to; in conclu-
  sion, equivocates him in a sleep, and, giving him the
  lie, leaves him.

Macduff

  I believe drink gave thee the lie last night.   35

Porter

  That it did, sir, i' the very throat on me; but I requited
  him for his lie; and, I think, being too strong for him,
  though he took up my legs sometime, yet I made a
  shift to cast him.

Macduff

  Is thy master stirring?   40

                 [Enter MACBETH.*]*

  Our knocking has awak'd him; here he comes.

Lennox

  Good morrow, noble sir!

Macbeth

                        Good morrow, both!

Macduff

  Is the King stirring, worthy Thane?

Macbeth

                                Not yet.

Macduff

  He did command me to call timely on him;

45. *slipped the hour* missed my appointment.

46–7. 'I know this is a duty that you take pleasure in. but still it is an inconvenience'. Macbeth replies in the elaborately polite style that he seems to use at times of strain.
48. *physics pain* acts as medicine to the pain (in this case the inconvenience) and removes it.

50. *limited* appointed. Macduff has already explained that the King had instructed him to wake him early.

53–60. Lennox's description of the wild weather clearly suggests a supernatural origin for it. Nature, in Shakespeare's work, often reflects tragic or horrible events in human life.

57–8. *Of dire combustion ... woeful time* Terrible confusion developing out of this dreadful time.
58–9. *the obscure bird ... night* the owl screamed right through the night.
59–60. *the earth Was feverous* the earth trembled (in an earthquake) like a man in a fever.

61–2. There has never been such a night in my comparatively short life.

63–4. Strictly speaking Macduff has the two subjects the wrong way round; what he means is 'The imagination cannot conceive such a horror and the tongue cannot express it'.

I have almost slipp'd the hour.   45
Macbeth
                        I'll bring you to him.
Macduff
  I know this is a joyful trouble to you;
  But yet 'tis one.
Macbeth
  The labour we delight in physics pain.
  This is the door.
Macduff
              I'll make so bold to call,
  For 'tis my limited service.   50

[Exit MACDUFF.*]*

Lennox
  Goes the King hence to-day?
Macbeth
  He does; he did appoint so.
Lennox
  The night has been unruly. Where we lay,
  Our chimneys were blown down; and, as they say,
  Lamentings heard i' th' air, strange screams of death,   55
  And prophesying, with accents terrible,
  Of dire combustion and confus'd events
  New hatch'd to th' woeful time; the obscure bird
  Clamour'd the livelong night. Some say the earth
  Was feverous and did shake.
Macbeth
                   'Twas a rough night.   60
Lennox
  My young remembrance cannot parallel
  A fellow to it.

[Re-enter MACDUFF.*]*

Macduff
  O horror, horror, horror! Tongue nor heart
  Cannot conceive nor name thee.

65. *Confusion* This was a very strong word, meaning something like utter chaos. This speech of Macduff's expresses the view of kingship as a powerful symbol of all order, linked to God, who created order in the first place.

67. *The Lord's anointed temple* Duncan, who like many kings, right down to the present day, was anointed with holy oil at his coronation.

71. *a new Gorgon* In the classical legend Medusa and her two sisters, all known as Gorgons, are represented as hideous women with snakes for hair who could turn to stone those who looked at them.

75. *downy sleep ... counterfeit* soft sleep, a gentle image of death.

77. *The great doom's image!* Macduff sees the murder of the King as comparable with the Day of Judgment at the end of the world.

78. *sprites* ghosts

81–2. That such a harsh trumpet calls those sleeping in the castle to a discussion (like opposing troops at a truce during war).

83–6. For the audience, there is a terrible irony in the idea of Lady Macbeth being too gentle and feminine to stand the awful news.

85. *repetition* report.

Macbeth and Lennox

What's the matter?

Macduff

 Confusion now hath made his masterpiece.   65
 Most sacrilegious murder hath broke ope
 The Lord's anointed temple, and stole thence
 The life o' th' building.

Macbeth

     What is't you say – the life?

Lennox

 Mean you his Majesty?

Macduff

 Approach the chamber, and destroy your sight 70
 With a new Gorgon. Do not bid me speak;
 See, and then speak yourselves.

[Exeunt MACBETH *and* LENNOX.*]*

     Awake, awake!
 Ring the alarum bell. Murder and treason!
 Banquo and Donalbain! Malcolm! awake!
 Shake off this downy sleep, death's counterfeit, 75
 And look on death itself. Up, up, and see
 The great doom's image! Malcolm! Banquo!
 As from your graves rise up and walk like sprites
 To countenance this horror! Ring the bell.

[Bell rings. Enter LADY MACBETH.*]*

Lady Macbeth

 What's the business,   80
 That such a hideous trumpet calls to parley
 The sleepers of the house? Speak, speak!

Macduff

 O gentle lady,
 'Tis not for you to hear what I can speak!
 The repetition in a woman's ear   85
 Would murder as it fell.

[Enter BANQUO.*]*

89. *What, in our house?* Does Lady Macbeth slip up in saying these words, or are they natural enough in the mouth of a supposedly horrified hostess?

91–6. Here is Macbeth's elaborate style again as though he had prepared the speech beforehand to prove how he feels.

91. *before this chance* before what has happened.

93. There's nothing worth attention in the whole of human activity.

94. *toys* triviality.

95–6. 'All the wine of life has been drawn from the cask and there is nothing but the dregs left', *(this vault* presumably the earth). The whole of this speech of Macbeth's has a dreadful irony about it. He is striving to act the part of a loyal, sorrowful subject but perhaps his words reveal his true feelings about what he's done and how it has changed him.

97. When Macbeth says the two young men are *amiss* he means they are ruined by their father's death.

98–9. *spring, head, fountain, source* all describe the place at which a river or stream commences. Macbeth is using four words which mean the same thing.

101–5. The Macbeths must be pleased that Lennox puts the blame on the grooms, but later it appears that this explanation doesn't satisfy everyone.

102. *badg'd* splotched (as though with red badges).

O Banquo, Banquo,
Our royal master's murder'd!

Lady Macbeth

Woe, alas!
What, in our house?

Banquo

Too cruel anywhere.
Dear Duff, I prithee contradict thyself,
And say it is not so.   90

[Re-enter MACBETH, LENNOX, with ROSS.]

Macbeth

Had I but died an hour before this chance,
I had liv'd a blessed time; for, from this instant,
There's nothing serious in mortality –
All is but toys; renown and grace is dead;
The wine of life is drawn, and the mere lees   95
Is left this vault to brag of.

[Enter MALCOLM and DONALBAIN.]

Donalbain

What is amiss?

Macbeth

You are, and do not know't.
The spring, the head, the fountain of your blood,
Is stopp'd; the very source of it is stopp'd.

Macduff

Your royal father's murder'd.

Malcolm

O, by whom?   100

Lennox

Those of his chamber, as it seem'd, had done't.
Their hands and faces were all badg'd with blood;
So were their daggers, which unwip'd we found
Upon their pillows. They star'd and were distracted;
No man's life was to be trusted with them.   105

107. Macduff seems to express particular puzzlement about Macbeth's killing the grooms. Perhaps his doubts about Macbeth's character start here.

108–18. Questioned so directly Macbeth makes great verbal efforts to sound convincing, but produces a string of very forced metaphors, and possibly only succeeds in convincing his wife that she must do something to draw attention away from him.

110. *expedition* rush.

111. *the pauser reason* reason, which causes a person to delay before acting.

116. *Unmannerly breech'd with gore* Macbeth is referring, in rather exaggerated language, to the daggers as though they had trousers of blood on them right up to the hilts. This is one of a large number of images from clothing in the play (see the Theme Index at the end).

116. *refrain* hold himself back (i.e. refrain from killing the grooms in righteous indignation).

118. Some think that Lady Macbeth's fainting-fit is put on in order to draw attention from her husband's over-acting; others regard it as the emotion and pressure having got to her – showing she is not as tough as she seems – and the beginning of her decline into madness.

120–1. Why are we keeping quiet, since we (Duncan's sons) have the best reason to express grief?

122. *auger-hole* an auger is the tool a carpenter uses for boring small holes. Donalbain is suggesting that their fate may be hidden nearby, ready to spring out and overwhelm them without warning (i.e. the murderer of their father may be prepared to kill them too). The expression also conveys the idea of the kind of hole made in a human body by a dagger.

124. People in the first shock of bereavement often find that they can't express their feelings freely by weeping. Donalbain is contrasting his own and his brother's reluctance to show their feelings with Macbeth's noisy display.

125. *Upon the foot of motion* ready to be expressed.

Macbeth
    O, yet I do repent me of my fury
    That I did kill them.
Macduff
                 Wherefore did you so?
Macbeth
    Who can be wise, amaz'd, temp'rate, and furious,
    Loyal and neutral, in a moment? No man.
    The expedition of my violent love   110
    Outrun the pauser reason. Here lay Duncan,
    His silver skin lac'd with his golden blood;
    And his gash'd stabs look'd like a breach in nature
    For ruin's wasteful entrance: there, the murderers,
    Steep'd in the colours of their trade, their daggers   115
    Unmannerly breech'd with gore. Who could refrain,
    That had a heart to love, and in that heart
    Courage to make's love known?
Lady Macbeth
                   Help me hence, ho!
Macduff
    Look to the lady.
Malcolm
    [aside to DONALBAIN*]* Why do we hold our tongues
        that most may claim   120
    This argument for ours?
Donalbain
    [aside to MALCOLM*]*   What should be spoken
    Here, where our fate, hid in an auger-hole,
    May rush and seize us? Let's away.
    Our tears are not yet brew'd.
Malcolm
    [aside to DONALBAIN*]*   Nor our strong sorrow
    Upon the foot of motion.
Banquo
                 Look to the lady.   125

    *[*LADY MACBETH *is carried out.]*

126. *naked frailties* unclothed, weak bodies

129. *scruples* doubts.

130–2. Banquo makes it clear that he is committed to an honest, open way of life, and he loathes the deceit *(undivulg'd pretence)* and hate *(malice)* that have killed Duncan. (Some critics think that Banquo is already fearful that Malcolm may soon be killed also, and that the *undivulg'd pretence* is the intention to destroy him.)

133. *manly readiness* either simply men's clothes (men may still be in their night-clothes) *or* masculine qualities such as courage and determination.

135. *consort* mix, associate.

136. *unfelt sorrow* This does not imply that Malcolm is unaffected by his father's death. The brothers have already agreed in lines 124–5 that they had not had time yet to be clear about their feelings and to express them.

136. *office* duty.

137. It is pretty clear that *the false man* is Macbeth, and that Malcolm and Donalbain know who their enemy is. *easy* easily.

138–9. *our separated fortune ... safer* 'we'll be safer if we stay apart'. But why?

139–40. *Where we are ... smiles* 'Here in Scotland those who smile at us (i.e. Macbeth) are really our deadly enemies'. Does this suggest that Macbeth has gone out of his way in this scene to appear friendly? If you were producing the play and wanted to make this point, where would you instruct Macbeth to smile?

140–1. *the near in blood ... bloody* those closest to us (Macbeth is a relative) may be the ones who are most murderous

141–2. *This murderous shaft ... lighted* An odd statement, because it has certainly *lighted* (fallen) once already, on Duncan. Malcolm means that it will hurt others before it has finished its flight.

144. *dainty of leave-taking* leave without ceremony.

145. *shift away* slip away secretly *(shift* here has the meaning of planning or contriving to do something).

145–6. *There's warrant ... left* Malcolm is a little uneasy about running away, but justifies it on the grounds that their enemy is ruthless. *steals* 'goes stealthily away' as well as 'robs'.

And when we have our naked frailties hid,
That suffer in exposure, let us meet,
And question this most bloody piece of work,
To know it further. Fears and scruples shake us.
In the great hand of God I stand, and thence   130
Against the undivulg'd pretence I fight
Of treasonous malice.

Macduff
                  And so do I.

All
                      So all.

Macbeth
Let's briefly put on manly readiness
And meet i' th' hall together.

All
                    Well contented.

[Exeunt all but MALCOLM and DONALBAIN.]

Malcolm
What will you do? Let's not consort with them.   135
To show an unfelt sorrow is an office
Which the false man does easy. I'll to England.

Donalbain
To Ireland I; our separated fortune
Shall keep us both the safer. Where we are,
There's daggers in men's smiles; the near in blood,   140
The nearer bloody.

Malcolm
            This murderous shaft that's shot
Hath not yet lighted; and our safest way
Is to avoid the aim. Therefore to horse;
And let us not be dainty of leave-taking,
But shift away. There's warrant in that theft   145
Which steals itself, when there's no mercy left.

[Exeunt.]

75

SCENE 4

Shakespeare frequently shows scenes in which strange and sinister events in Nature reflect human horrors and disasters. The disturbing things that Ross and the Old Man tell us about emphasize the unnaturalness of Macbeth's crime. Another purpose of the scene is to present Macduff as a decent man (he is referred to as *the good Macduff*) who strongly suspects Macbeth and is unwilling go to Scone for Macbeth's coronation (line 36).

Stage Direction *Without* outside. When Macduff enters he comes straight from the castle with the latest news.

1. *Threescore and ten* the traditional life-span of a man is 70 years, so this Old Man, who must be nearly 80, looks back with particular authority; even he can recall nothing like the night that has just passed.

3–4. *this sore night ... knowings* this terrible night has made all previous experiences seem trivial.

6. *his bloody stage* the stage on which man carries out his bloody deeds – that is, the earth.

7. *strangles the travelling lamp* obscures the sun.

12–13. *tow'ring* and *place* terms from falconry, *towering* means spiralling upwards to the place or 'pitch', which was the height from which a hawk 'stooped' or swooped down on to its prey. For an owl to attack and kill a falcon would have been unusual

13. *mousing* hunting mice.

15. *minions* favourites – that is, the best of their kind.

16. *Turn'd wild in nature* went back to being wild – no longer domestic animals.

17. *as* as if.

18. *eat* the past tense, now spelt 'ate'.

Scene 4

Inverness. Without Macbeth's castle

[Enter ROSS *with an* OLD MAN.*]*

Old Man
    Threescore and ten I can remember well;
    Within the volume of which time I have seen
    Hours dreadful and things strange; but this sore night
    Hath trifled former knowings.

Ross
                Ah, good father,
    Thou seest, the heavens, as troubled with man's act,   5
    Threatens his bloody stage. By th' clock 'tis day,
    And yet dark night strangles the travelling lamp.
    Is't night's predominance, or the day's shame,
    That darkness does the face of earth entomb,
    When living light should kiss it?

Old Man
                   'Tis unnatural,   10
    Even like the deed that's done. On Tuesday last,
    A falcon, tow'ring in her pride of place,
    Was by a mousing owl hawk'd at and kill'd.

Ross
    And Duncan's horses – a thing most strange and
        certain –
    Beauteous and swift, the minions of their race,   15
    Turn'd wild in nature, broke their stalls, flung out,
    Contending 'gainst obedience, as they would make
    War with mankind.

Old Man
              'Tis said they eat each other.

Ross
    They did so; to the amazement of mine eyes,
    That look'd upon't.

23. Macduff is careful at first to only say what is being said officially, but before the end of the scene it becomes evident that he has, privately, other ideas.

24. *pretend* intend.

24. *suborn'd* paid to do the deed.

27. *'Gainst nature still* Yet another unnatural event!

28. *Thriftless* unprofitable.

28. *ravin up* 'wolf down', swallow greedily.

29. *Thine own life's means* the source of their own life, i.e. their father.

29. *like* likely.

30. New kings of Scotland were appointed by a form of election.

31. *Scone* the ancient royal city; kings were crowned on the Stone of Destiny, which was supposed to be Jacob's pillow (see *Genesis* 28, verse 11). In 1296 Edward I of England took the stone to Westminster Abbey and, since then, all British sovereigns have been crowned on it.

32. *To be invested* to go through the coronation ceremony.

33. *Colmekill* The name means Colm's, or St Columba's, cell, on the island of Iona; this was where Scottish kings were buried.

34. *The sacred … predecessors* the place where previous kings had been buried.

36. *Fife* the home of Macduff, Thane of Fife.

[Enter MACDUFF.]

                Here comes the good Macduff.   20
How goes the world, sir, now?

Macduff

                      Why, see you not?

Ross

Is't known who did this more than bloody deed?

Macduff

Those that Macbeth hath slain.

Ross

                    Alas, the day!
What good could they pretend?

Macduff

                    They were suborn'd
Malcolm and Donalbain, the King's two sons,   25
Are stol'n away and fled; which puts upon them
Suspicion of the deed.

Ross

                'Gainst nature still.
Thriftless ambition, that wilt ravin up
Thine own life's means! Then 'tis most like
The sovereignty will fall upon Macbeth.   30

Macduff

IIe is already nam'd, and gone to Scone
To be invested.

Ross

            Where is Duncan's body?

Macduff

Carried to Colmekill,
The sacred storehouse of his predecessors
And guardian of their bones.

Ross

                Will you to Scone?   35

Macduff

No, cousin, I'll to Fife.

37. *Well* Macduff repeats, probably sarcastically, Ross's neutral-sounding '*Well*'

40. *benison* blessing.
40–1. The Old Man's hopes are the first suggestion of a possible reversal of fortunes in the future. So far only those who have turned good into bad have been successful.

Ross

                    Well, I will thither.

Macduff

    Well, may you see things well done there! Adieu,
    Lest our old robes sit easier than our new.

Ross

    Farewell, father.

Old Man

    God's benison go with you, and with those   40
    That would make good of bad, and friends of foes.

[Exeunt.]

ACT 3 SCENE 1

Banquo is now almost certain that Macbeth became king by foul means. He, too, would like to have the witches' prophecies about him fulfilled, but apparently has no intention of using Macbeth's methods. Do you think he should have been more actively anti-Macbeth? Does Banquo strike you as someone with the right ideas, but without the determination to go through with them? Or is he, in his own way as ambitious as Macbeth?

4. *It should ... posterity* Your descendants would not become kings.
6. *them* the witches.
7. *their speeches shine* their words come gloriously true.
8. *verities* truths.
9. *oracles* An oracle, among the Greeks and Romans, was a person who acted as a mouthpiece of the gods. Banquo wonders whether the witches do perhaps tell the truth, and whether what they said about him may prove reliable.
10. *But, hush, no more* Banquo dismisses his own ambitious thoughts.

Stage Direction *Sennet sounded* a sennet was a series of notes on a trumpet, announcing an important arrival, such as that of a king.

11–13. Macbeth begins by deliberately flattering Banquo, and Lady Macbeth joins in with even more flowery language (there is an ominous echo of the Macbeths' invitation to Duncan).

13. *all-thing unbecoming* totally unfitting.
14. *solemn* formal (the word usually means this in Shakespeare).

15–18. The style of Banquo's response seems as artificial as the invitation. Do you blame him for this? (It is possible that, when he says *Let your Highness Command upon me,* he means 'If you, as King, order me, I haven't much alternative'. At least this may be what he implies.)

ACT 3
Scene 1

Forres. The palace

[Enter BANQUO.]

Banquo
Thou hast it now – King, Cawdor, Glamis, all
As the weird women promis'd; and I fear
Thou play'dst most foully for't; yet it was said
It should not stand in thy posterity;
But that myself should be the root and father   5
Of many kings. If there come truth from them –
As upon thee, Macbeth, their speeches shine –
Why, by the verities on thee made good,
May they not be my oracles as well
And set me up in hope? But, hush, no more.   10

[Sennet sounded. Enter MACBETH as King, LADY MACBETH as Queen; LENNOX, ROSS, LORDS, LADIES and ATTENDANTS.]

Macbeth
Here's our chief guest.
Lady Macbeth
            If he had been forgotten,
It had been as a gap in our great feast,
And all-thing unbecoming.
Macbeth
To-night we hold a solemn supper, sir,
And I'll request your presence.
Banquo
              Let your Highness   15
Command upon me; to the which my duties
Are with a most indissoluble tie
For ever knit.

19. The reason for this question, and the ones in lines 23 and 35, will soon become obvious. They are put privately to Banquo; the rest of the court should not hear them.

21. *which still ... prosperous* Which has always been well-considered and productive.
22. *but we'll take to-morrow* I, the King, will have to hear your advice tomorrow instead.

25. *this* now.
25–7. *Go not my horse ... twain* Unless my horse goes faster (than usual), it will have been dark for an hour by the time I get back.

29. *are bestow'd* have settled.

31. *parricide* killing a father.
32. The *strange invention* is the idea ('invented' according to Macbeth) by Malcolm and Donalbain that Macbeth was the murderer of their father. Some time has now gone by and the sons have no doubt been trying to gain support abroad by giving their version of what had happened.
33. *therewithal* besides that.
33–4. *cause of state ... jointly* state affairs which will require our combined attention.
34. *Hie you* Hurry.
36. *our time does call upon's* we should be going.

40–3. You're all free to do as you wish until seven o'clock this evening; I will remain unattended until supper-time, so that human company will be all the pleasanter then.
43. *While* Until.

Macbeth
Ride you this afternoon?
Banquo
              Ay, my good lord.
Macbeth
We should have else desir'd your good advice –   20
Which still hath been both grave and prosperous –
In this day's council; but we'll take to-morrow.
Is't far you ride?
Banquo
As far, my lord, as will fill up the time
Twixt this and supper. Go not my horse the better,   25
I must become a borrower of the night
For a dark hour or twain.
Macbeth
             Fail not our feast.
Banquo
My lord, I will not.
Macbeth
We hear our bloody cousins are bestow'd
In England and in Ireland, not confessing   30
Their cruel parricide, filling their hearers
With strange invention; but of that to-morrow,
When therewithal we shall have cause of state
Craving us jointly. Hie you to horse; adieu,
Till you return at night. Goes Fleance with you?   35
Banquo
Ay, my good lord; our time does call upon's.
Macbeth
I wish your horses swift and sure of foot,
And so I do commend you to their backs.
Farewell. *[Exit* BANQUO*]*
Let every man be master of his time   40
Till seven at night; to make society
The sweeter welcome, we will keep ourself
Till supper-time alone. While then. God be with you!

44. *Attend those men our pleasure?* 'Are those men waiting for me?' (Macbeth must already have mentioned them to his servant.)

45. *without* outside.

46–7. *To be thus ... safely thus* Just being king is nothing; to be safely established on the throne is what's important.

48. *Stick deep* Are like thorns (or daggers) sticking in my flesh.

48. *royalty of nature* Banquo was the ancestor of later Scottish (and English) kings, but the word *royalty* also suggests Macbeth envies Banquo's noble and firm character, qualities he lacks.

50. *to* in addition to.

51–2. *He hath a wisdom ... in safety* We have seen this prudent side of Banquo earlier in the scene. Can you recall an occasion when he showed his *dauntless temper*?

53–5. *under him ... by Caesar* This refers to an old belief that one man's 'guardian angel' might be overcome by another's, resulting in the first man's destruction. The Caesar referred to is Octavius Caesar who, although a younger man, defeated Mark Antony.

55. *chid* literally 'scolded', but 'spoke sternly to' might be better.

59. *fruitless crown* 'a crown that I would not be able to pass on'.

60. *barren sceptre* in the next line is an exactly parallel phrase. *Crown* and *sceptre* were the two main symbols of kingship.

61. *with an unlineal hand* 'by the hand of someone unrelated to me'. Macbeth hates the idea of someone else's son becoming king after him.

63. *fil'd* defiled.

65. *rancours* bitterness and hatred.

65–8. The *vessel* Macbeth has in mind may be the communion cup, because he goes on in religious terms.

66. *eternal jewel* his immortal soul.

67. *the common enemy of man* the Devil. What he can't bear is that he has thrown away his own hope of salvation in order to put Banquo's descendants *(seeds)* on the Scottish throne.

69–70. Roughly, Macbeth is saying, 'I'd rather fight Fate itself to the bitter end' as if in a medieval tournament. The *list* was the enclosure in which such tournaments were held, to *champion* was to challenge, and 'a l'outrance' *(to th' utterance)* meant 'until one of the contestants died'.

[Exeunt all but MACBETH *and a* SERVANT.*]*

Sirrah, a word with you. Attend those men our pleasure?

Servant
    They are, my lord, without the palace gate.   45
Macbeth
    Bring them before us. *[Exit* SERVANT*]* To be thus is nothing,
    But to be safely thus. Our fears in Banquo
    Stick deep; and in his royalty of nature
    Reigns that which would be fear'd. 'Tis much he dares,
    And to that dauntless temper of his mind   50
    He hath a wisdom that doth guide his valour
    To act in safety. There is none but he
    Whose being I do fear; and under him
    My Genius is rebuk'd, as it is said
    Mark Antony's was by Caesar. He chid the Sisters   55
    When first they put the name of King upon me,
    And bade them speak to him; then prophet-like,
    They hail'd him father to a line of kings.
    Upon my head they plac'd a fruitless crown
    And put a barren sceptre in my gripe,   60
    Thence to be wrench'd with an unlineal hand,
    No son of mine succeeding. If't be so,
    For Banquo's issue have I fil'd my mind;
    For them the gracious Duncan have I murder'd;
    Put rancours in the vessel of my peace   65
    Only for them, and mine eternal jewel
    Given to the common enemy of man
    To make them kings – the seeds of Banquo kings!
    Rather than so, come. Fate, into the list,
    And champion me to th' utterance! Who's there?   70

[Re-enter SERVANT *and two* MURDERERS.*]*

Now go to the door and stay there till we call.

[Exit SERVANT.*]*

72–140. Macbeth goes to great lengths to persuade the murderers to kill Banquo. It seems (see lines 73–82) that he has previously told them that Banquo is responsible for their lack of success, not himself as they had believed. In fact, they grudgingly accept that Banquo had persecuted them personally. (*You made it known to us,* line 82). Macbeth then goes on to bully them verbally, as his wife bullied him not long before (Act 1, Scene 7, lines 35–59) by questioning their manhood and eventually they give in to the pressure.

75–6. *which held you So under fortune* who held you down lower than you deserve.

77–8. *I made good to you ... pass'd in probation with you* Both phrases mean 'I proved to you'.

79. *How you were borne in hand* What tricks of deceit were practised on you.

79. *how cross'd* how you were frustrated.

79. *the instruments* what means were used.

80. *Who wrought with them* who used those means.

84–9. *Do you find ... for ever?* Patience and Christian forgiveness are presented as contemptible weaknesses. Note that the thing which is now bothering Macbeth most is mentioned here; Banquo's *issue* (children).

91–106. In this astonishing tirade about dogs of various kinds Macbeth argues that all kinds of dogs have their special functions in Nature's orderly arrangement, yet he is using the argument to persuade the men to destroy the human order by becoming murderers.

92. *Shoughs* shaggy northern dogs.

92. *water-rugs* rough water-dogs.

92. *demi-wolves* the offspring of dogs and wolves – perhaps something like huskies

92. *clept* called.

93. *The valued file* The list in which their various qualities are set down.

95. *The house-keeper* what we would call 'a good house-dog', one that can be relied upon to keep intruders away.

96–7. *the gift ... in him clos'd* the particular ability which generous Nature has enclosed in him (or endued him with).

97–9. *whereby he does receive ... all alike* by which he receives a special quality that distinguishes him in the general category 'dog'.

Was it not yesterday we spoke together?

First Murderer

It was, so please your Highness.

Macbeth

Well then, now
Have you consider' d of my speeches? Know
That it was he, in the times past, which held you   75
So under fortune; which you thought had been
Our innocent self. This I made good to you
In our last conference, pass'd in probation with you,
How you were borne in hand, how cross'd, the
          instruments,
Who wrought with them, and all things else that
          might   80
To half a soul and to a notion craz'd
Say 'Thus did Banquo.'

First Murderer

You made it known to us.

Macbeth

I did so; and went further, which is now
Our point of second meeting. Do you find
Your patience so predominant in your nature   85
That you can let this go? Are you so gospell'd,
To pray for this good man and for his issue,
Whose heavy hand hath bow'd you to the grave
And beggar'd yours for ever?

First Murderer

We are men, my liege.

Macbeth

Ay, in the catalogue ye go for men;   90
As hounds, and greyhounds, mongrels, spaniels, curs,
Shoughs, water-rugs, and demi-wolves, are clept
All by the name of dogs. The valued file
Distinguishes the swift, the slow, the subtle,
The house-keeper, the hunter, every one   95
According to the gift which bounteous nature
Hath in him clos'd; whereby he does receive

102–4. *And I will … us* I will reveal the secret details of the plan the execution of which will destroy your enemy and make me your ally.

105–6. Macbeth declares that, as long as Banquo is alive, he cannot enjoy life like a healthy man. He is also suggesting that he is in constant danger from Banquo.

110. *tugg'd with fortune* 'pushed around by fortune', as in a wrestling match.
112. *To mend it or be rid on't* To improve my life or to put an end to it.

114. *in such bloody distance* in such deadly rivalry.
115–16. *every minute … near'st of life* 'every minute that he's alive I'm in desperate danger' (*thrusts Against my near'st of life* suggests a sword about to enter a vital part of the body).
117. *bare-fac'd power* naked force.
118. *bid my will avouch it* say that he is being destroyed simply because I feel like it.
119. *For* Because of.
120. *Whose loves … drop* Whose respect and affection I don't want to lose.
120–1. *but wail … struck down* but I must instead mourn the death of the man I myself destroyed.
122. That I make such strong appeals for your assistance.

Particular addition, from the bill
That writes them all alike; and so of men,
Now, if you have a station in the file,   100
Not i' th' worst rank of manhood, sayt;
And I will put that business in your bosoms
Whose execution takes your enemy off,
Grapples you to the heart and love of us,
Who wear our health but sickly in his life,   105
Which in his death were perfect.

Second Murderer

                                          I am one, my liege,
Whom the vile blows and buffets of the world
Hath so incens'd that I am reckless what
I do to spite the world.

First Murderer

                              And I another,
So weary with disasters, tugg'd with fortune,   110
That I would set my life on any chance,
To mend it or be rid on't.

Macbeth

                              Both of you
Know Banquo was your enemy.

Both Murderers

                                        True, my lord.

Macbeth

So is he mine; and in such bloody distance
That every minute of his being thrusts   115
Against my near'st of life; and though I could
With bare-fac'd power sweep him from my sight,
And bid my will avouch it, yet I must not,
For certain friends that are both his and mine,
Whose loves I may not drop, but wail his fall   120
Who I myself struck down. And thence it is
That I to your assistance do make love,
Masking the business from the common eye
For sundry weighty reasons.

128. This is a puzzle. Some people think the mysterious Third Murderer who joins the other two at the beginning of Act 3, Scene 3 is this *perfect spy o' th' time* . But it's more likely that the phrase means 'the exact, or best guess of the time you will be needed'.

130. *something from the palace* a certain distance from the palace.

130–1. *always thought ... a clearness* you must fully understand that I cannot be linked to the crime in any way.

131. *him* Banquo.

132. *no rubs nor botches* 'no imperfections or errors' (they must make a completely successful job of it).

134. *material* important.

136. *Resolve yourselves apart* Go away and make up your minds.

138. *I'll call upon you straight* I shall require your services very soon.

Second Murderer
                        We shall, my lord,
  Perform what you command us.
First Murderer
                       Though our lives –   125
Macbeth
  Your spirits shine through you. Within this hour at most,
  I will advise you where to plant yourselves,
  Acquaint you with the perfect spy o' th' time,
  The moment on't; for 't must be done to-night,
  And something from the palace; always thought   130
  That I require a clearness; and with him,
  To leave no rubs nor botches in the work,
  Fleance his son, that keeps him company,
  Whose absence is no less material to me
  Than is his father's, must embrace the fate   135
  Of that dark hour. Resolve yourselves apart;
  I'll come to you anon.
Both Murderers
                    We are resolv'd, my lord.
Macbeth
  I'll call upon you straight; abide within.

[Exeunt MURDERERS.*]*

  It is concluded: Banquo, thy soul's flight
  If it find heaven must find it out to-night.   140

[Exit.]

SCENE 2

This scene shows a striking change in the relationship between Macbeth and his wife. They are both disillusioned about the power and position they have gained at so great a cost; they both say that it's better to be dead than suffer the misery they are going through now. However, this is about all they agree on. Lady Macbeth seems almost fatalistic ('what's done is done...') while Macbeth is desperately planning more crimes in order to protect his position and wipe out the possibility of Banquo's descendants inheriting the throne.

1. Lady Macbeth's first words suggest that she suspects her husband is plotting Banquo's death, but he has not told her about it.
3–4. *I would ... a few words* I should like to speak to him when he is free.

4–5. *Nought's had ... content* We have done our utmost and achieved nothing; we've got what we wanted, but it has given us no happiness.
6–7. She seems almost to envy the dead Duncan and she says that the murder has not brought her any steady contentment.
9. With your own miserable fantasies as your only form of company.

10–11. *those thoughts ... they think on* the fearful thoughts (of murder) should have stopped as soon as the murder was accomplished.

13. *scotch'd* slashed (i.e. cut without killing).
14. *close* join up again, healed itself.
14–15. *our poor malice ... former tooth*: our feeble ability to do harm is vulnerable to its regained power.

16. *But let the frame ... suffer* 'But let the whole universe collapse, and heaven and earth be destroyed ...'

Scene 2

Forres. The palace

[Enter LADY MACBETH and a SERVANT.]

Lady Macbeth
Is Banquo gone from court?

Servant
Ay, madam, but returns again to-night.

Lady Macbeth
Say to the King I would attend his leisure
For a few words.

Servant
                    Madam, I will.

[Exit.]

Lady Macbeth
                              Nought's had, all's spent,
Where our desire is got without content.   5
'Tis safer to be that which we destroy,
Than by destruction dwell in doubtful joy.

[Enter MACBETH.]

How now, my lord! Why do you keep alone,
Of sorriest fancies your companions making,
Using those thoughts which should indeed have died   10
With them they think on? Things without all remedy
Should be without regard. What's done is done.

Macbeth
We have scotch'd the snake, not kill'd it;
She'll close, and be herself, whilst our poor malice
Remains in danger of her former tooth.   15
But let the frame of things disjoint, both the
        worlds suffer,
Ere we will eat our meal in fear and sleep

19–22. *Better be … restless ecstasy* Macbeth, without realizing it, repeats Lady Macbeth's thought in lines 6–7.

21. The image here is of a rack used to torture people.
22. *ecstasy* frenzy, a state of mental turmoil.

24–6. *nor steel … touch him further* assassination attempts with weapon or poison, rebellion at home, attack from abroad – none of these now has the power to disturb Duncan.

27. *Gentle my lord* It was quite common in Shakespeare's time to put the adjective in this position. The modern order is, of course, 'My gentle lord'.
27. *sleek o'er your rugged looks* smooth away your worried looks.
30. Be particularly attentive to Banquo.
31. *Present him eminence* Honour him in your speech.
32. *Unsafe the while … what they are* We are so unsafe at the moment that we must preserve our honour by flattering others, and mask our true feelings.

35. *You must leave this* You must stop thinking like this.
38. Since Fleance is still very young, this certainly sounds like a hint to Macbeth that he can kill him (the 'copy' of his father?) and Banquo too. They are mortal (part of 'Nature'), and can die. Or perhaps she is probing to discover whether Macbeth is already committed to murdering them.
39. With her encouragement, Macbeth temporarily regains the feeling of partnership in hideous crime with his wife, and speaks of the planned murders in much the same way as he spoke of Duncan's as it approached – with disgust and yet with a kind of relish.
40. *jocund* joyful.
41. *cloister'd flight* because bats often live in church buildings and can be seen flying in the cloisters in the evening.
42. *shard–borne* the expression could mean either carried on wings like shards (pieces of pottery) or born in cow-dung. The second is the more likely meaning.
43. *night's yawning peal* the curfew-bell which announces the time for sleep.

In the affliction of these terrible dreams
That shake us nightly. Better be with the dead,
Whom we, to gain our peace, have sent to peace,   20
Than on the torture of the mind to lie
In restless ecstasy. Duncan is in his grave;
After life's fitful fever he sleeps well;
Treason has done his worst; nor steel, nor poison,
Malice domestic, foreign levy, nothing,   25
Can touch him further.

Lady Macbeth
                              Come on.
Gentle my lord, sleek o'er your rugged looks;
Be bright and jovial among your guests to-night.

Macbeth
So shall I, love; and so, I pray, be you.
Let your remembrance apply to Banquo;   30
Present him eminence, both with eye and tongue –
Unsafe the while, that we
Must lave our honours in these flattering streams,
And make our faces vizards to our hearts,
Disguising what they are.

Lady Macbeth
                              You must leave this.   35

Macbeth
O, full of scorpions is my mind, dear wife!
Thou know'st that Banquo, and his Fleance, lives.

Lady Macbeth
But in them nature's copy's not eterne.

Macbeth
There's comfort yet; they are assailable.
Then be thou jocund. Ere the bat hath flown   40
His cloister'd flight; ere to black Hecate's summons
The shard-borne beetle with his drowsy hums
Hath rung night's yawning peal, there shall be done
A deed of dreadful note.

Lady Macbeth
                              What's to be done?

46–7. *Come … day* Macbeth is appealing to the night to hide his fearful crime from the light as falconers used to stitch together *(seel)* the eyes of a hawk when training it.

49–50. *that great bond … pale* what Shakespeare probably had in mind was the divine law against murder. Most moral laws seem to make Macbeth *pale* and fearful.

50. *thickens* grows dim.

50–1. *the crow … rooky wood* the crow (or rook) flies to its wood, which is already black with many birds.

55. Macbeth seems to be getting his conscience under control, 'When one has done something evil to begin with, strength and security are gained by further evil'. The words seem to be said as some sort of reassurance: practice makes perfect, in evil as well as in good.

Macbeth
    Be innocent of the knowledge, dearest chuck,   45
    Till thou applaud the deed. Come, seeling night,
    Scarf up the tender eye of pitiful day,
    And with thy bloody and invisible hand
    Cancel and tear to pieces that great bond
    Which keeps me pale. Light thickens, and the crow   50
    Makes wing to th' rooky wood;
    Good things of day begin to droop and drowse,
    Whiles night's black agents to their preys do rouse.
    Thou marvell'st at my words; but hold thee still:
    Things bad begun make strong themselves by ill.   55
    So, prithee go with me.

              [Exeunt.]

SCENE 3

The appearance of an unexpected Third Murderer perhaps gives us more insight into Macbeth's present state of mind. He is so full of suspicion that he sends another villain to check up on his hired thugs. Between them, the three are more than enough for Banquo, but Fleance manages to escape.

2–4. We need not be suspicious (of this newcomer) since he has just given us instructions which are exactly like those Macbeth gave us himself.

6. *lated traveller* one who is still journeying as night comes on.
7. *timely inn* the inn he reaches just in time (before night is fully come).
8. *The subject of our watch* Banquo.

10. *That ... expectation* That are expected (i.e. on the guest-list).

11. *go about* take a roundabout route.
12–14. The whole murder-plan depends on the fact that people who arrive at the castle usually leave their horses with grooms and walk the last few hundred yards.

Scene 3

Forres. The approaches to the palace

[Enter three MURDERERS.*]*

First Murderer
But who did bid thee join with us?
Third Murderer
                              Macbeth.
Second Murderer
He needs not our mistrust, since he delivers
Our offices, and what we have to do,
To the direction just.
First Murderer
                    Then stand with us.
The west yet glimmers with some streaks of day;   5
Now spurs the lated traveller apace
To gain the timely inn, and near approaches
The subject of our watch.
Third Murderer
                        Hark! I hear horses.
Banquo
[within] Give us a light there, ho!
Second Murderer
                        Then 'tis he; the rest
That are within the note of expectation   10
Already are i' th' court.
First Murderer
                        His horses go about.
Third Murderer
Almost a mile; but he does usually,
So all men do, from hence to th' palace gate
Make it their walk.

        [Enter BANQUO, *and* FLEANCE *with a torch.]*

101

15. *Stand to 't* Be at the ready to do the deed.

16. With black humour the First Murderer answers Banquo's comment on the weather with a remark that also refers to the rain of blows he and the others immediately deliver.

19. *Was't not the way*? Wasn't it the right thing to do?

20–1. Macbeth's emphasis on the need to kill Fleance as well as Banquo has clearly impressed itself on the murderers.

Second Murderer
A light, a light!
Third Murderer
     'Tis he.
First Murderer
Stand to 't.   15
Banquo
It will be rain to-night.
First Murderer
       Let it come down.

     [Stabs BANQUO.*]*

Banquo
O, treachery! Fly, good Fleance, fly, fly, fly.
Thou mayst revenge. O slave!

     [Dies. FLEANCE *escapes.]*

Third Murderer
Who did strike out the light?
First Murderer
          Was't not the way?
Third Murderer
There's but one down; the son is fled.
Second Murderer
           We have lost   20
Best half of our affair.
First Murderer
      Well, let's away,
And say how much is done.

      [Exeunt.]

SCENE 4

Macbeth organised the second murder with far less anxiety than for the murder of Duncan but, during this scene, he once again loses control of himself and shows extreme fear. Are these the same sort of misgivings as he showed over Duncan? By the end of the scene how has he regained control? Has Lady Macbeth's help been vital, or does Macbeth finally control his feelings without her assistance?

The scene can be quite simply staged, with thrones for Macbeth and his wife and a large table for the state banquet. Banquo's ghost is sometimes presented with scientific ingenuity, using mirrors, but nothing of this kind was attempted in Shakespeare's theatre. What method would you choose if you were directing a modern production?

1. *degrees* respective rank, or seniority. This would determine where the guests sat at table.
2. From the beginning to the end of the banquet you are all heartily welcome.
4. *society* the assembled guests.
6. *keeps her state* stays seated on her throne. *in best time* at the right time.
7. *require her welcome* request her to welcome you.

11. There seem to be equal numbers on both sides of the table. Where is it that Macbeth decides to sit (*i'th' midst*)?
12. *large* generous (Macbeth encourages them to enjoy themselves freely, and to show it).
13. Macbeth sees one of the murderers at the door and moves over to speak to him.
15. 'I prefer the blood to be outside you, not inside him'; another example of Macbeth's peculiarly grim humour.

Scene 4

Forres. The palace

[Banquet prepared. Enter MACBETH, LADY MACBETH, ROSS, LENNOX, LORDS *and* ATTENDANTS.]

Macbeth
  You know your own degrees, sit down.
  At first and last the hearty welcome.
Lords
  Thanks to your Majesty.
Macbeth
  Our self will mingle with society
  And play the humble host.   5
  Our hostess keeps her state; but in best time
  We will require her welcome.
Lady Macbeth
  Pronounce it for me, sir, to all our friends;
  For my heart speaks they are welcome.

[Enter FIRST MURDERER *to the door.]*

Macbeth
  See, they encounter thee with their hearts' thanks.   10
  Both sides are even; here I'll sit i' th' midst.
  Be large in mirth; anon we'll drink a measure
  The table round. *[Going to the door]*
  There's blood upon thy face.
Murderer
                     'Tis Banquo's then.
Macbeth
  'Tis better thee without than he within.   15
  Is he despatch'd?
Murderer
            My lord, his throat is cut;
  That I did for him.
Macbeth
             Thou art the best o' th' cut-throats;

19. *the nonpareil* the very best.

21. *fit* spasm of fear.
21. *perfect* Macbeth seems to be continuing the health metaphor he used earlier (Act 3, Scene 1, lines 105–6).
22. *Whole* firm.
22. *founded* immovable.
23. As unlimited and free as the surrounding air.
24. *cabin'd, cribb'd, confin'd* all these words mean 'shut up in a small space'. The alliteration produces emphasis.
25. *saucy* impudent.
27. *trenched* deeply cut.
28. The least of the cuts enough to kill a man.

29. *worm* snake.
30. Will naturally, in time, develop the power to poison.
31–2. *to-morrow ... again* 'we'll meet and discuss the matter in detail'.

33. *give the cheer* 'give encouragement' (as a host should) or possibly 'propose a toast'.

37. *Sweet remembrancer!* Macbeth is thanking his wife for reminding him of his duties as host.

Yet he's good that did the like for Fleance.
If thou didst it, thou art the nonpareil.
Murderer
    Most royal sir – Fleance is 'scap'd.   20
Macbeth
    Then comes my fit again. I had else been perfect,
    Whole as the marble, founded as the rock,
    As broad and general as the casing air,
    But now I am cabin'd, cribb'd, confin'd, bound in
    To saucy doubts and fears. But Banquo's safe?   25
Murderer
    Ay, my good lord. Safe in a ditch he bides,
    With twenty trenched gashes on his head,
    The least a death to nature.
Macbeth
                    Thanks for that.
    There the grown serpent lies; the worm that's fled
    Hath nature that in time will venom breed,   30
    No teeth for th' present. Get thee gone; to-morrow
    We'll hear, ourselves, again.

          [Exit MURDERER.*]*

Lady Macbeth
                  My royal lord,
    You do not give the cheer; the feast is sold
    That is not often vouch'd, while 'tis a-making,
    'Tis given with welcome. To feed were best at home: 35
    From thence the sauce to meat is ceremony;
    Meeting were bare without it.

[Enter the GHOST OF BANQUO *and sits in* MACBETH'S *place.]*

Macbeth
                  Sweet remembrancer!
    Now good digestion wait on appetite,
    And health on both!

40. *our country's honour* Macbeth's deliberately exaggerated way of referring to Banquo.

41. *grac'd* gracious.

42–3. Macbeth, with terrible insincerity, says that he hopes he can blame Banquo for bad manners, rather than feel anxious because ill fortune may have prevented him from attending.

43–4. *His absence ... promise* He shouldn't have said he was going to be present if he couldn't manage it.

46. Macbeth glances round the table and merely registers the fact that the seat he intended to sit in (the one *i'th' midst*) is now occupied. He doesn't at first see that Banquo's ghost is occupying it.

49. *Which of you have done this?* What does this mean? Is it possible that Macbeth really suspects that someone has tried to trick him by staging the appearance of Banquo's ghost? Or does he mean: 'Which of you killed Banquo?'

50–1. Macbeth rejects the idea that he is responsible because he says he didn't actually do the killing himself.

52–5. Ross's remark about Macbeth's apparent illness gives Lady Macbeth an opportunity to make up a fairly convincing explanation on the spur of the moment.

55. *upon a thought* in a moment.

56–7. If you take a great deal of notice of him you will only annoy him and enrage him even more.

58. *Are you a man?* Lady Macbeth's main method to snap Macbeth out of his 'fit' is the 'Pull yourself together' one, shaming him with her contemptuous comments.

Lennox
                    May't please your Highness sit?

Macbeth
    Here had we now our country's honour roof'd,   40
    Were the grac'd person of our Banquo present;
    Who may I rather challenge for unkindness
    Thank pity for mischance.

Ross
                            His absence, sir,
    Lays blame upon his promise. Please 't your Highness
    To grace us with your royal company.   45

Macbeth
    The table's full.

Lennox
                    Here is a place reserv'd, sir.

Macbeth
    Where?

Lennox
                                Here, my good lord.
    What is't that moves your Highness?

Macbeth
    Which of you have done this?

Lords
                            What, my good lord?

Macbeth
    Thou canst not say I did it; never shake   50
    Thy gory locks at me.

Ross
    Gentlemen, rise; his Highness is not well.

Lady Macbeth
    Sit, worthy friends. My lord is often thus,
    And hath been from his youth. Pray you, keep seat.
    The fit is momentary; upon a thought   55
    He will again be well. If much you note him,
    You shall offend him and extend his passion.
    Feed, and regard him not.—Are you a man?

60. *O proper stuff!* What you're saying is sheer rubbish!

61. *painting of your fear* an imaginary vision brought about by fear, not real at all.

62. *air-drawn* drawn in the air (and therefore unreal).

63. *flaws and starts* wild fits. *flaw* a sudden squall.

64. *Impostors to true fear* again, she means 'not the real thing' – his frightened behaviour isn't based on anything that would properly inspire fear.

65–6. *A woman's ... grandam* An old wives' tale passed down from a previous generation.

66. *Shame itself!* You are the personification of shame.

69. *how say you?* there, what do you say to that? It's making gestures now!

70. *nod* This often meant 'beckon' in Shakespeare's time. Perhaps Banquo's ghost is inviting Macbeth to join him in death.

71–3. *If charnel-houses ... kites* 'If men come back from the dead like this, the only way to dispose of a body completely will be to feed it to kites.' (Kites were common scavenger-birds in earlier times in England, as they still are in other parts of the world.)

71. *charnel-houses* stores of bones dug up by grave-diggers.

73. *maws* stomachs.

73. *unmanned* unmanly

74. *Fie* Shame!

76–80. *Ere humane statute ... an end* 'Murders were committed in previous ages, before civilized laws cleansed society and made it more gentle, and they have been committed in more recent times, too – murders too horrible to describe – but in the past the murdered men died when their brains were knocked out, and that was the end of them.

81. *twenty mortal murders* see lines 27–8. *twenty trenched gashes ... The least a death to nature.*

81. *crowns* heads.

82. *strange* the word here, and in many other places in the play, means something like 'unnatural'.

Macbeth
  Ay, and a bold one that dare look on that
  Which might appal the devil.
Lady Macbeth
                              O proper stuff!   60
  This is the very painting of your fear;
  This is the air-drawn dagger which you said
  Led you to Duncan. O, these flaws and starts –
  Impostors to true fear – would well become
  A woman's story at a winter's fire,   65
  Authoriz'd by her grandam. Shame itself!
  Why do you make such faces? When all's done,
  You look but on a stool.
Macbeth
                          Prithee see there.
  Behold! look! lo! how say you?
  Why, what care I? If thou canst nod, speak, too.   70
  If charnel-houses and our graves must send
  Those that we bury back, our monuments
  Shall be the maws of kites. *[Exit* GHOST*]*
Lady Macbeth
                          What, quite unmann'd in folly?
Macbeth
  If I stand here, I saw him.
Lady Macbeth
                          Fie, for shame!
Macbeth
  Blood hath been shed ere now, i' th' olden time,   75
  Ere humane statute purg'd the gentle weal;
  Ay, and since too, murders have been perform'd
  Too terrible for the ear. The time has been
  That when the brains were out the man would die,
  And there an end; but now they rise again,   80
  With twenty mortal murders on their crowns,
  And push us from our stools. This is more strange
  Than such a murder is.

85. *muse at me* be astonished at me.

88. *Then I'll sit down* when the health has been drunk.

89–93. No one but Macbeth sees the ghost. Do you think, then, that it is a fantasy present only in Macbeth's mind? Should it be visible to the audience?

91. *we thirst* we desire to drink.

92. *all to all* let us all drink to each other.

92. *Our duties, and the pledge* We offer our respects (to your Majesty) and drink the toast (you propose).

93. *Avaunt* go away. At this moment all the lords are on their feet, ready to drink the toast. When Macbeth's fit comes again, no doubt they remain standing, stunned. Then, perhaps, they mutter among themselves as he continues to rave.

93–4. *Let the earth ... cold* you're a corpse; you should be in a grave.

95. *speculation* light of intelligence.

97. *a thing of custom* a quite normal happening.

99. Macbeth continues to address the ghost, oblivious of Lady Macbeth's attempt to calm the horrified lords. Nevertheless he is partly answering her charge of not being a man.

100. If you came in the form of a shaggy Russian bear.

101. *arm'd* i.e. with a horn.

101. *Hyrcan tiger* a tiger from Hyrcania, a region near the Caspian Sea.

102. *but that* except the form of the dead Banquo.

104. Challenge me to fight with swords by ourselves in the desert.

105. *inhabit* stay at home. *protest* declare.

106. *The baby of a girl* a baby girl.

107. Lady Macbeth's insistence on the unreality of what he sees has had some effect on him. As soon as he asserts that the ghost is *Unreal*, it disappears.

Lady Macbeth
                            My worthy lord,
  Your noble friends do lack you.
Macbeth
                                I do forget.
  Do not muse at me, my most worthy friends;   85
  I have a strange infirmity, which is nothing
  To those that know me. Come, love and health to all;
  Then I'll sit down. Give me some wine, fill full.

                [Enter GHOST.*]*

  I drink to the general joy o' th' whole table,
  And to our dear friend Banquo, whom we miss.   90
  Would he were here! To all, and him, we thirst,
  And all to all.
Lords
                     Our duties, and the pledge.
Macbeth
  Avaunt, and quit my sight. Let the earth hide thee.
  Thy bones are marrowless, thy blood is cold;
  Thou hast no speculation in those eyes   95
  Which thou dost glare with!
Lady Macbeth
                       Think of this, good peers,
  But as a thing of custom. 'Tis no other;
  Only it spoils the pleasure of the time.
Macbeth
  What man dare, I dare.
  Approach thou like the rugged Russian bear,   100
  The arm'd rhinoceros, or th' Hyrcan tiger;
  Take any shape but that, and my firm nerves
  Shall never tremble. Or be alive again,
  And dare me to the desert with thy sword;
  If trembling I inhabit, then protest me   105
  The baby of a girl. Hence, horrible shadow!
  Unreal mock'ry, hence!

107. *being gone* now that it has gone.

109–10. You have destroyed the good humour and shattered a pleasant social occasion with mad behaviour that has astounded everyone.

111. *overcome* pass over.
112–13. *You make me strange ... owe* 'You (i.e. all those present) make me doubtful of my own nature.' (Because he is deeply frightened, while they seem undisturbed by what he saw.)
113. *I owe* that belongs to me.

116. *mine is blanch'd* my natural colour *(ruby)* has been replaced by paleness.

118–20. *Question enrages him ...* It is clear that Lady Macbeth is not going to allow her husband to incriminate himself any further. She makes sure that they all leave without delay.
118. *At once, good night* Let me say good-night to all of you together.
119. Don't bother about who is most senior as you leave.

121. As soon as she has ushered them all out she seems to be nervously exhausted. Her handling of this very difficult situation is in fact the last sign of her control of things.

122. *It* the murder of Banquo, or perhaps Banquo's ghost itself.

124–6. *Augurs ... man of blood* Drawing conclusions from omens.
125. *maggot-pies* magpies, *choughs* crows or jackdaws. The augurs, or Roman priests, often made predictions from what they observed of birds in flight.
126. *What is the night?* What time of night is it?

[Exit GHOST.*]*

            Why, so; being gone,
I am a man again. Pray you, sit still.

Lady Macbeth
   You have displac'd the mirth, broke the good meeting,
   With most admir'd disorder.

Macbeth
                    Can such things be,   110
   And overcome us like a summer's cloud,
   Without our special wonder? You make me strange
   Even to the disposition that I owe,
   When now I think you can behold such sights
   And keep the natural ruby of your cheeks,   115
   When mine is blanch'd with fear.

Ross
                 What sights, my lord?

Lady Macbeth
   I pray you speak not; he grows worse and worse;
   Question enrages him. At once, good night.
   Stand not upon the order of your going,
   But go at once.

Lennox
           Good night; and better health   120
   Attend his Majesty!

Lady Macbeth
          A kind good night to all!

[Exeunt LORDS *and* ATTENDANTS.*]*

Macbeth
   It will have blood; they say blood will have blood.
   Stones have been known to move, and trees to speak;
   Augurs and understood relations have
   By maggot-pies and choughs and rooks brought
       forth   125
   The secret'st man of blood. What is the night?

127. *Almost at odds with morning* 'It's hard to say whether it's night or morning.' It has been pointed out that this is a symbolic moment, the centre point of the play, when the darkness represented by Macbeth is for the first time about to begin to fade as signs of opposition (representing a new dawn) are about to appear (notice Macduff's defiance, referred to in the next line).

131–2. Macbeth employs spies in the houses of all his thanes. The picture of a cruel dictatorship maintained by fear in an atmosphere of suspicion becomes more complete.

133. *betimes* early, very soon.

134. *bent* determined.

135–6. *For mine own good ... give way* Everything else must take second place to my welfare.

136–8. The image is, appropriately, of wading across a river of blood. He feels he is already wading so deeply that he may as well go on to the far side.

139–40. I have dark thoughts that will become deeds – the sort that have to be put into effect without being carefully considered first.

142–3. *My strange and self-abuse ... hard use* Those strange fantasies I thought I saw were merely the fears of a beginner lacking tough practice.

144. *We* the royal 'we' refers to Macbeth himself, as Lady Macbeth is now no longer part of his planning.

Lady Macbeth
    Almost at odds with morning, which is which.
Macbeth
    How say'st thou that Macduff denies his person
    At our great bidding?
Lady Macbeth
                         Did you send to him, sir?
Macbeth
    I hear it by the way; but I will send –   130
    There's not a one of them but in his house
    I keep a servant fee'd – I will to-morrow.
    And betimes I will to the Weird Sisters:
    More shall they speak; for now I am bent to know
    By the worst means the worst. For mine own good   135
    All causes shall give way. I am in blood
    Stepp'd in so far that, should I wade no more,
    Returning were as tedious as go o'er.
    Strange things I have in head that will to hand,
    Which must be acted ere they may be scann'd.   140
Lady Macbeth
    You lack the season of all natures, sleep.
Macbeth
    Come, well to sleep. My strange and self-abuse
    Is the initiate fear that wants hard use.
    We are yet but young in deed.

                    [Exeunt.]

117

SCENE 5

It is unlikely that Shakespeare wrote this scene. The rhythm and style are quite different from those of the earlier scenes with the witches. Hecate's introduction into the play serves little purpose and the scene is usually cut in modern productions.

1. *Hecat* (or Hecate) a goddess of witchcraft in Greek mythology.
1. *angerly* angrily or, as we would say, 'angry'.
2. *beldams* hags, hideous old women.

6. *charms* magical powers.
7. Secret organiser of wickedness.

11. *wayward son* unreliable pupil.

15. *pit of Acheron* apparently the name of the witches' cave (*Acheron* was one of the rivers of Hell in classical legend).

20. *I am for th' air* 'I am going up into the air' (like the traditional witch on a broomstick).
21. *Unto a dismal ... end* On a disastrous and ominous purpose.
23–9. It was believed that the moon shed a kind of dew on certain plants, and this liquid was highly prized for its magic qualities.
24. *vap'rous drop profound* a drop of vapour with profound powers.

26. *sleights* arts.

27. *artificial sprites* spirits or apparitions conjured up by magic arts.

29. *confusion* ruin.

Scene 5

A heath

[Thunder. Enter the three WITCHES, *meeting* HECATE.]

First Witch
    Why, how now, Hecat! You look angerly.
Hecate
    Have I not reason, beldams as you are,
    Saucy and overbold? How did you dare
    To trade and traffic with Macbeth
    In riddles and affairs of death; 5
    And I, the mistress of your charms,
    The close contriver of all harms,
    Was never call'd to bear my part,
    Or show the glory of our art?
    And, which is worse, all you have done 10
    Hath been but for a wayward son,
    Spiteful and wrathful; who, as others do,
    Loves for his own ends, not for you.
    But make amends now. Get you gone,
    And at the pit of Acheron 15
    Meet me i' the morning; thither he
    Will come to know his destiny.
    Your vessels and your spells provide,
    Your charms, and everything beside.
    I am for th' air; this night I'll spend 20
    Unto a dismal and a fatal end.
    Great business must be wrought ere noon.
    Upon the corner of the moon
    There hangs a vap'rous drop profound;
    I'll catch it ere it come to ground; 25
    And that, distill'd by magic sleights,
    Shall raise such artificial sprites
    As, by the strength of their illusion,
    Shall draw him on to his confusion.

30–1. *bear/His hopes ... fear* he will become utterly careless of considerations such as commonsense. God's grace and natural fear, (swept away by the wild hopes the witches will give him.)
32. *security* over-confidence.

Stage Direction This song occurs in a play called *The Witch* by Middleton, a contemporary of Shakespeare.
34–5. *little spirit* Hecate's familiar.

He shall spurn fate, scorn death, and bear   30
His hopes 'bove wisdom, grace, and fear;
And you all know security
Is mortals' chiefest enemy.

[Music and a song within: 'Come away, come away, etc.']

Hark! I am call'd; my little spirit, see,
Sits in a foggy cloud, and stays for me.   35

[Exit.]

First Witch
Come, let's make haste; she'll soon be back again.

[Exeunt.]

SCENE 6

Since his last words in the Banquet Scene *(Good night; and better health Attend his Majesty!)* Lennox has obviously done some hard thinking. The deep irony of some of his remarks is very striking. Apart from the fact that some of the Scottish lords have now 'seen through' Macbeth, the scene provides the first real suggestion of better things to come.

1–3. *My former speeches ... borne* The remarks I have recently made have only put into words what you were thinking already. You can work out things in greater detail for yourself. All I say is that things have been carried on in a very odd way.

3–4. *The gracious Duncan ... Macbeth* The suggestion is that Macbeth could afford to pity Duncan when he was dead.

5–7. Macbeth had put the blame for Duncan's death on Malcolm and Donalbain, because they had fled to England. Lennox sarcastically suggests that it's just as reasonable to say that Fleance killed his father, as he has fled, too.

8–10. Who can help thinking how unnatural it was for Malcolm and Donalbain to kill their own father?

10. *fact* evil deed.

11. *straight* immediately.

12. *pious* loyal, patriotic.

12. *delinquents* those who have failed in their duty.

13. *thralls* can also mean slaves.

14–16. *Ay, and wisely ... men deny't* Without saying so, Lennox makes it clear that Macbeth was wise to kill the guards because they might have been able to convince people of their innocence.

17. *He has borne all things well* He has organized everything with remarkable skill.

18. *under his key* locked up.

19. *an't* if it.

20. Again very sarcastically, Lennox says that Macbeth would teach Malcolm, Donalbain and Fleance a lesson for killing their fathers (the 'lesson' being death!)

21. *broad* outspoken

23–4. *can you tell ... himself?* do you know where he's staying?

24–5. *The son of Duncan ... birth* Malcolm, from whom the dictator Macbeth withholds his rightful inheritance (the throne of Scotland).

Scene 6

Forres. The palace

[Enter LENNOX and another LORD.]

Lennox

My former speeches have but hit your thoughts,
Which can interpret farther. Only I say
Things have been strangely borne. The gracious Duncan
Was pitied of Macbeth. Marry, he was dead.
And the right-valiant Banquo walk'd too late;   5
Whom, you may say, ift please you, Fleance kill'd,
For Fleance fled. Men must not walk too late.
Who cannot want the thought how monstrous
It was for Malcolm and for Donalbain
To kill their gracious father? Damned fact!   10
How it did grieve Macbeth! Did he not straight,
In pious rage, the two delinquents tear,
That were the slaves of drink and thralls of sleep?
Was not that nobly done? Ay, and wisely too;
For 'twould have anger'd any heart alive   15
To hear the men deny't. So that, I say,
He has borne all things well; and I do think
That had he Duncan's sons under his key –
As, an't please heaven, he shall not – they should find
What 'twere to kill a father; so should Fleance.   20
But peace! For from broad words, and 'cause he fail'd
His presence at the tyrant's feast, I hear,
Macduff lives in disgrace. Sir, can you tell
Where he bestows himself?

Lord

       The son of Duncan,
From whom this tyrant holds the due of birth,   25
Lives in the English court, and is receiv'd
Of the most pious Edward with such grace
That the malevolence of fortune nothing

28–9. *That the malevolence ... respect* the fact that he's had such ill fortune doesn't reduce in any way the honour he receives (in the English court).

30. *the holy King* Edward the Confessor, seen as holy and pious.

31. *wake* rouse. The Earl of Northumberland is later called 'Old Siward' and his *warlike* son 'Young Siward'.

32–3. *with Him above To ratify the work* with God to strengthen their activities.

34–6. Have good food on our tables again, sleep well at night, hold banquets without the fear of bloody murder, pay sincere respect to a rightful king and receive from him honours freely earned ...

38. *exasperate* exasperated, irritated.

40–3. Macbeth sent for Macduff, as he told Lady Macbeth he would (Act 3, Scene 4, line 130), but Macduff flatly rejected the summons *(Sir, not I!)*; the surly *(cloudy)* messenger turned his back on Macduff and grunted, as if to say 'You'll live to regret burdening me with such an answer' (which suggests anyone who brought an unsatisfactory message to Macbeth was likely to suffer for it).

43–5. *And that well might ... provide* That should be enough to warn Macduff to stay as far away as possible from Macbeth.

47. *His* Macduff's.

48–9. *our suffering country ... accursed!* our country, now suffering under a damned tyranny.

Takes from his high respect; thither Macduff
Is gone to pray the holy King upon his aid   30
To wake Northumberland and warlike Siward,
That by the help of these – with Him above
To ratify the work – we may again
Give to our tables meat, sleep to our nights,
Free from our feasts and banquets bloody knives,   35
Do faithful homage and receive free honours –
All which we pine for now. And this report
Hath so exasperate the King that he
Prepares for some attempt of war.

Lennox
                             Sent he to Macduff?

Lord
He did; and with an absolute 'Sir, not I!'   40
The cloudy messenger turns me his back
And hums, as who should say 'You'll rue the time
That clogs me with this answer'.

Lennox
                           And that well might
Advise him to a caution t' hold what distance
His wisdom can provide. Some holy angel   45
Fly to the court of England and unfold
His message ere he come, that a swift blessing
May soon return to this our suffering country
Under a hand accurs'd!

Lord I'll send my prayers with him.

[Exeunt.]

ACT 4 SCENE 1

The appearance of the witches in Act 1, Scene 3, set in motion Macbeth's first steps in crime; now he seeks them out and they introduce his deeper and much more desperate involvement in evil.

1. *brinded* streaked. This cat (perhaps what we should call a tabby) is the First Witch's familiar, called Graymalkin, Act 1, Scene 1, line 9.
2. *hedge-pig* hedgehog.

3. *Harpier* the Third Witch's familiar. This is probably the mythical monster, a harpy, a creature with a woman's face and body and a bird's wings and claws. *Harpier* screams, and the Third Witch announces this as the signal to begin.

6–8. The toad has, while sleeping, sweated poison *(swelter'd venom sleeping got)* for 31 days and nights.

12. A slice of marsh-snake.

16. *fork* the forked tongue.
16. *blind-worm's sting* we know now that the blind-worm, or slow-worm, is not poisonous, but there was a firm belief in Shakespeare's time that it was.
17. *howlet's wing* owl's wing.
19. The witch commands the filthy mixture to seethe and gain evil power.

ACT 4
Scene 1

A dark cave. In the middle, a cauldron boiling

[Thunder. Enter the three WITCHES.]

First Witch
  Thrice the brinded cat hath mew'd.
Second Witch
  Thrice and once the hedge-pig whin'd.
Third Witch
  Harpier cries; 'tis time, 'tis time.
First Witch
  Round about the cauldron go;
  In the poison'd entrails throw.   5
  Toad that under cold stone
  Days and nights has thirty-one
  Swelter'd venom sleeping got
  Boil thou first i th' charmed pot.
All
  Double, double toil and trouble;   10
  Fire burn, and cauldron bubble.
Second Witch
  Fillet of a fenny snake,
  In the cauldron boil and bake;
  Eye of newt, and toe of frog,
  Wool of bat, and tongue of dog,   15
  Adder's fork, and blind-worm's sting,
  Lizard's leg, and howlet's wing—
  For a charm of pow'rful trouble,
  Like a hell-broth boil and bubble.
All
  Double, double toil and trouble;   20
Third Witch
  Scale of dragon, tooth of wolf,

22. *Witch's mummy* dried flesh from a witch's body. (Dried human flesh was thought to have medicinal and magical powers.)

22. *maw and gulf* throat and stomach.

23. *ravin'd* stuffed with the flesh of its human victim.

24. The hemlock plant is in any case poisonous; digging it up at night was supposed to increase its powers.

25–30. The Jew, the Turk, the Tartar and the baby strangled at birth would all be seen in Shakespeare's time as anti-Christian or non-Christian, and certainly un-christened.

26. *slips of yew* cuttings from a yew-tree, which is associated with churchyards and is also poisonous (cattle sometimes become ill through eating yew-leaves).

27. Cut off during an eclipse of the moon (considered a time of misfortune to the superstitious).

30. Born to a prostitute, in a ditch.

31. *gruel;* a soupy mixture.

31. *slab* slimy and sticky.

32. *tiger's chaudron* a tiger's guts.

33. *ingredience* we would write 'ingredients'.

38–42. It is unlikely that these lines and stage directions are by Shakespeare.

43. There is an old superstition that sudden unexpected pains are omens of coming events.

Witch's mummy, maw and gulf
Of the ravin'd salt-sea shark,
Root of hemlock digged i' th' dark,
Liver of blaspheming Jew,   25
Gall of goat, and slips of yew
Sliver'd in the moon's eclipse,
Nose of Turk, and Tartar's lips,
Finger of birth-strangled babe
Ditch-deliver'd by a drab –   30
Make the gruel thick and slab;
Add thereto a tiger's chaudron,
For th' ingredience of our cauldron.

All
Double, double toil and trouble;
Fire burn, and cauldron bubble.   35

Second Witch
Cool it with a baboon's blood,
Then the charm is firm and good.

[Enter HECATE.]

Hecate
O well done! I commend your pains;
And every one shall share i' th' gains.
And now about the cauldron sing,   40
Like elves and fairies in a ring,
Enchanting all that you put in.

[Music and a song: 'Black Spirits, etc.' Exit HECATE]

Second Witch
By the pricking of my thumbs,
Something wicked this way comes. *[Knocking]*
Open, locks, whoever knocks.   45

[Enter MACBETH.]

Macbeth
How now, you secret, black, and midnight hags!

47. *A deed ... name* It's too horrible to be described.

48. I call upon you in the name of your devilish art

50–1. *let them fight ... churches* again, the anti-Christian nature of witchcraft is emphasized.

51. *yesty* frothing, like fermenting yeast.

52. *swallow navigation up* wreck ships.

53. *Though bladed corn be lodg'd* though the corn is blown flat even before the ears are formed.

54. *their warders' heads* the heads of those who guard them.

55–6. *Slope ... foundations* bend down to their bases, i.e. are blown flat.

56–7. *Though ... together* Macbeth's obsessive interest in his own position has now gone to extremes. He has reached the desperate state of a crazy dictator who doesn't mind if the universe is destroyed as long as he gets his own way.

57. *nature's germens* the very seeds of life.

58. *till destruction sicken* destruction is personified as a violent man who finally becomes disgusted by his own deeds, like one who eats so much that he makes himself sick.

61. *our masters* the devils whom the witches serve.

63. *farrow* piglets (the number 9 – 3 times 3 – was particularly potent in magic).

63. *sweaten* sweated, oozed out.

64. *gibbet* gallows.

66. Show yourself, and at the same time go through your performance efficiently.

Macbeth

                What is't you do?

All

  A deed without a name.

Macbeth

  I conjure you by that which you profess –
  Howe'er you come to know it – answer me.
  Though you untie the winds and let them fight   50
  Against the churches; though the yesty waves
  Confound and swallow navigation up;
  Though bladed corn be lodg'd and trees blown down;
  Though castles topple on their warders' heads;
  Though palaces and pyramids do slope   55
  Their heads to their foundations; though the treasure
  Of nature's germens tumble all together,
  Even till destruction sicken – answer me
  To what I ask you.

First Witch

           Speak.

Second Witch

             Demand.

Third Witch

                We'll answer.

First Witch

  Say, if thou'dst rather hear it from our mouths,   60
  Or from our masters?

Macbeth

            Call 'em; let me see 'em.

First Witch

  Pour in sow's blood that hath eaten
  Her nine farrow; grease that's sweaten
  From the murderer's gibbet throw
  Into the flame.

All

          Come, high or low;   65
  Thyself and office deftly show.

Stage Direction The **Armed Head** might well be the helmeted head of Macbeth as it is when Macduff cuts it off later. However, for the moment it has no special meaning for Macbeth (*thou unknown power*, line 67).

72. harp'd guessed.

Stage Direction The **Bloody Child** is Macduff as a baby from his mother's womb *untimely ripp'd* (Act 5, Scene 8, lines 15–16).

76. Had I three ears ... Macbeth's grim humour suggests that he retains some of his old confidence; later he falls into a state of hopelessness

82. take a bond of fate hold Fate itself to its word, by killing Macduff.
83. So that I can prove that my weak fears are unjustified.
84. He hears the thunder of the Stage Direction as he speaks. Thunder was often regarded as the voice of an angry god.
Stage Direction The **Child Crowned** is probably Malcolm, who later orders his troops to use branches from Birnam Wood as camouflage.

85. issue child.

[Thunder. FIRST APPARITION, an Armed Head.]
Macbeth
  Tell me, thou unknown power –
First Witch
                            He knows thy thought.
  Hear his speech, but say thou nought.
Apparition
  Macbeth! Macbeth! Macbeth! Beware Macduff;
  Beware the Thane of Fife. Dismiss me. Enough.   70

[He descends.]

Macbeth
  Whate'er thou art, for thy good caution, thanks;
  Thou hast harp'd my fear aright. But one word more –
First Witch
  He will not be commanded. Here's another,
  More potent than the first.

[Thunder. SECOND APPARITION, a Bloody Child.]

Apparition
  Macbeth! Macbeth! Macbeth! Macbeth   75
  Had I three ears, I'd hear thee.
Apparition
  Be bloody, bold, and resolute; laugh to scorn
  The pow'r of man, for none of woman born
  Shall harm Macbeth. *[Descends]*
Macbeth
  Then live, Macduff; what need I fear of thee?   80
  But yet I'll make assurance double sure
  And take a bond of fate. Thou shalt not live;
  That I may tell pale-hearted fear it lies,
  And sleep in spite of thunder.

[Thunder. THIRD APPARITION, a Child Crowned, with a tree
in his hand.]

                  What is this
  That rises like the issue of a king,   85

86–7. *round And top* a very Shakespearian phrase, full of meaning. A crown is literally round and is worn on top of the head, but also (especially in Macbeth's eyes) it is metaphorically the 'rounding-off' and summit of all ambition.

89. *Who chafes, who frets* who rages and storms.

91. Birnam and Dunsinane are about twelve miles apart. You may think that Shakespeare gives the impression that they are much closer than this in Act 5.

92. *That will never be* Macbeth takes the apparitions' words very literally and unquestioningly. Perhaps he simply dares not take them otherwise?

93. *impress* conscript, i.e. make the trees march.

94. *bodements* prophecies.

95. *Rebellion's head* the forces which may rise to remove Macbeth from the throne.

97. *Shall live the lease of nature* a complete human lifetime

97–8. *pay his breath ... custom* stop breathing in the course of time, i.e. die a natural death.

100–1. After a show of returning confidence Macbeth cannot resist asking the question regarding Fleance's escape which has grown in his mind; 'Have I committed these crimes merely for another man's sons to inherit the throne?'

Stage Direction *Hautboys* the hautboy was a high-pitched wooden instrument, as the name suggests. The modern form of the word is 'oboe'.

104. *noise* music.

And wears upon his baby brow the round
And top of sovereignty?
All
                          Listen, but speak not to't.
Apparition
  Be lion-mettled, proud, and take no care
  Who chafes, who frets, or where conspirers are:
  Macbeth shall never vanquish'd be until   90
  Great Birnam wood to high Dunsinane Hill
  Shall come against him. *[Descends]*
Macbeth
                      That will never be
  Who can impress the forest, bid the tree
  Unfix his earth-bound root? Sweet bodements, good!
  Rebellion's head rise never till the wood   95
  Of Birnam rise, and our high-plac'd Macbeth
  Shall live the lease of nature, pay his breath
  To time and mortal custom. Yet my heart
  Throbs to know one thing; tell me, if your art
  Can tell so much – shall Banquo's issue ever   100
  Reign in this kingdom?
All
                      Seek to know no more.
Macbeth
  I will be satisfied. Deny me this,
  And an eternal curse fall on you! Let me know.
  Why sinks that cauldron? And what noise is this?

                  [Hautboys.]

First Witch
  Show!   105
Second Witch
  Show!
Third Witch
  Show!
All
  Show his eyes, and grieve his heart;

Stage Direction *A Show of eight Kings* a dumb–show, or mime, was a regular feature in plays of Shakespeare's time. In this one Banquo mocks Macbeth by introducing him to a line of eight Stuart kings who are all descendants of his. This seems to be roughly historically accurate, except that there is no mention of Mary, Queen of Scots. During the show Macbeth goes through a variety of strong emotions, horror, rage, despair and finally blank depression.

111. *thy hair* This probably means 'your general appearance or character'.

114. *Start, eyes* Macbeth would rather that his eyes should pop from his head than that he should see any more.

115. *th' crack of doom* Doomsday, the moment when the world will come to an end.

117–19. The mirror carried by the eighth shows Macbeth many Banquo-like figures, including some who carry *two-fold balls* (double orbs representing the union of England and Scotland) and *treble sceptres* (signifying rule over England, Scotland and Ireland). Such a description applied to James I, who was descended from Banquo, and who probably saw the play at some time.

121. *blood-bolter'd* with hair plastered in blood.

128. *antic round* grotesque dance.

129–30. It is possible that these words were really addressed to James I seated in the audience or perhaps they are an ironic comment on Macbeth.

131–2. Macbeth is getting into the habit of uttering hideous but empty curses.

133. It is interesting to note that Lennox still serves Macbeth, in spite of the doubts he expressed about him in Act 3, Scene 6.

Come like shadows, so depart!

[A Show of eight Kings, and BANQUO *last; the last king*
with a glass in his hand.]

Macbeth

Thou art too like the spirit of Banquo; down!   110
Thy crown does sear mine eye-balls. And thy hair,
Thou other gold-bound brow, is like the first.
A third is like the former. Filthy hags!
Why do you show me this? A fourth? Start, eyes.
What, will the line stretch out to th' crack of doom?   115
Another yet? A seventh? I'll see no more.
And yet the eighth appears, who bears a glass
Which shows me many more; and some I see
That two-fold balls and treble sceptres carry.
Horrible sight! Now I see 'tis true;   120
For the blood-bolter'd Banquo smiles upon me,
And points at them for his. *[The show vanishes]*
        What! is this so?

First Witch

Ay, sir, all this is so. But why
Stands Macbeth thus amazedly?
Come, sisters, cheer we up his sprites,   125
And show the best of our delights;
I'll charm the air to give a sound,
While you perform your antic round;
That this great king may kindly say,
Our duties did his welcome pay.   130

[Music. The WITCHES *dance, and vanish.]*

Macbeth

Where are they? Gone? Let this pernicious hour
Stand aye accursed in the calendar.
Come in, without there.

[Enter LENNOX.*]*

Lennox

                        What's your Grace's will?

136–7. More curses!

139–40. Macbeth is shocked that the prophecies seem already to be making sense.

142. Time is holding him back – he was planning to kill Macduff, but he has escaped to England.

143–4. 'The only way of making sure that an intention becomes reality is to act as soon as you think of it'. In the next sentence Macbeth resolves to go one better; to act on emotion *(firstlings of my heart)* without thinking purposefully at all.

148. *surprise* take by surprise.

151. *trace* follow.

Macbeth
  Saw you the Weird Sisters?
Lennox
                  No, my lord.
Macbeth
  Came they not by you?
Lennox
               No, indeed, my lord.   135
Macbeth
  Infected be the air whereon they ride;
  And damn'd all those that trust them! I did hear
  The galloping of horse. Who was't came by?
Lennox
  'Tis two or three, my lord, that bring you word
  Macduff is fled to England.
Macbeth
                Fled to England!   140
Lennox
  Ay, my good lord.
Macbeth
  [aside] Time, thou anticipat'st my dread exploits.
  The flighty purpose never is o'ertook
  Unless the deed go with it. From this moment
  The very firstlings of my heart shall be   145
  The firstlings of my hand. And even now,
  To crown my thoughts with acts, be it thought
      and done
  The castle of Macduff I will surprise,
  Seize upon Fife, give to the edge o' th' sword
  His wife, his babes, and all unfortunate souls   150
  That trace him in his line. No boasting like a fool:
  This deed I'll do before this purpose cool.
  But no more sights! – Where are these gentlemen?
  Come, bring me where they are.   155

           [Exeunt.]

SCENE 2

Macduff has fled to England, without telling his wife. She is naturally bitter about this, and seems to think he is a coward. It is often suggested that he went secretly so that Macbeth would have no excuse for harming his wife and children. Examine the evidence as it comes out and try to decide whether Macduff's action is justifiable. And how are we to view Ross and the Messenger, here? Yes, they seem to warn Lady Macduff, but could they have done more? Or are they just ordinary decent men bewildered by an evil political regime.

3–4. *When our actions ... traitors* Lady Macduff thinks that her husband has not actually plotted against Macbeth, but that he has fled through fear and as a result laid himself open to the charge of treachery.

7. *titles* his estates and possessions.
9. *He wants the natural touch* a terrible accusation from a wife, equivalent to saying 'he hasn't any normal feelings of love and protectiveness'. Does she really mean this?
10. *most diminutive* tiniest.
12–14. 'His fear for his own skin has driven out all love for his family. What's more, the same fear has driven out all sense, too; what reason is there for such a flight ?' This gives Ross his cue to suggest that Macduff may have very good reasons for fleeing.
14. *coz* an affectionate term, applied in a variety of relationships.
15. *school* control.
15. *for* as for, concerning.
17. *The fits o' th' season* the violent disturbances of the time.
18–19. *when we are traitors ... ourselves* when we're regarded as traitors without knowing it.
19–20. *when we hold rumour ... fear* when we believe the stories we hear, because we're afraid, without knowing what there is to be afraid of.
22. *Each way and none* the general idea seems to be that frightened people are tossed backwards and forwards on the sea of fear without getting anywhere.

Scene 2

Fife. Macduff's castle

[Enter LADY MACDUFF, *her* SON, *and* ROSS.]

Lady Macduff
What had he done to make him fly the land?
Ross
You must have patience, madam.
Lady Macduff
                   He had none;
His flight was madness. When our actions do not,
Our fears do make us traitors.
Ross
                You know not
Whether it was his wisdom or his fear. 5
Lady Macduff
Wisdom! To leave his wife, to leave his babes,
His mansion, and his titles, in a place
From whence himself does fly? He loves us not;
He wants the natural touch; for the poor wren,
The most diminutive of birds, will fight, 10
Her young ones in her nest, against the owl.
All is the fear, and nothing is the love;
As little is the wisdom, where the flight
So runs against all reason,
Ross
             My dearest coz,
I pray you, school yourself. But, for your husband, 15
He is noble, wise, judicious, and best knows
The fits o' th' season. I dare not speak much further;
But cruel are the times, when we are traitors
And do not know ourselves; when we hold rumour
From what we fear, yet know not what we fear, 20
But float upon a wild and violent sea
Each way and none. I take my leave of you;

24–5. Ross's wise remark suggests to the audience that some change in fortune may be about to occur.

28–9. Ross means that he feels like crying and would embarrass Lady Macduff by doing so if he stayed any longer.

30–63. Macduff's small son, with his precocious questions and answers, provides an interval of partly comic Shakespearian 'back-chat' which brings out the horror of the end of the scene.
30. *Sirrah* a term used by parents to children (and also by masters to servants).
30. *dead* as good as dead. She doesn't expect to see him again.

34. *lime* bird-lime, a sticky substance spread to catch birds.
35. *The pitfall ... the gin* two other methods of catching birds – a disguised hole in the ground (presumably for flightless birds) and a snare.
36. *Poor birds ... for* the boy is saying, shrewdly, 'If I'm a poor bird, as you say, I'm in no danger; no one's silly enough to set traps for *poor* birds!'

41. *Then you'll buy ...* If they're as easy to get as all that, they won't be worth keeping.

    Shall not be long but I'll be here again.
    Things at the worst will cease, or else climb upward
    To what they were before. – My pretty cousin,   25
    Blessing upon you!
Lady Macduff
    Father'd he is, and yet he's fatherless.
Ross
    I am so much a fool, should I stay longer,
    It would be my disgrace and your discomfort.
    I take my leave at once.

                        [Exit.]

Lady Macduff
                        Sirrah, your father's dead;   30
    And what will you do now? How will you live?
Son
    As birds do, mother.
Lady Macduff
                        What, with worms and flies?
Son
    With what I get, I mean; and so do they.
Lady Macduff
    Poor bird! thou'dst never fear the net nor lime,
    The pitfall nor the gin.   35
Son
    Why should I, mother? Poor birds they are not set for.
    My father is not dead, for all your saying.
Lady Macduff
    Yes, he is dead. How wilt thou do for a father?
Son
    Nay, how will you do for a husband?
Lady Macduff
    Why, I can buy me twenty at any market.   40
Son
    Then you'll buy 'em to sell again.

42–3. ***Thou speak'st ... thee*** You're not talking very sensibly – but perhaps sensibly enough, considering how young you are.

45. She is probably referring to her husband's running away and leaving her, which she sees as treachery. In line 47 she suggests that he has broken his marriage-vow by leaving her.

55. ***enow*** enough.

57. ***poor monkey!*** an affectionate phrase, showing her amusement at her son's clever chatter. But immediately after it she becomes sad and serious again.

Lady Macduff
Thou speak'st with all thy wit; and yet, i' faith,
With wit enough for thee.
Son
Was my father a traitor, mother?
Lady Macduff
Ay, that he was.   45
Son
What is a traitor?
Lady Macduff
Why, one that swears and lies.
Son
And be all traitors that do so?
Lady Macduff
Every one that does so is a traitor, and must be
        hang'd.
Son
And must they all be hang'd that swear and lie?   50
Lady Macduff
Every one.
Son
Who must hang them?
Lady Macduff
Why, the honest men.
Son
Then the liars and swearers are fools; for there are
liars and swearers enow to beat the honest men and   55
hang up them.
Lady Macduff
Now, God help thee, poor monkey! But how wilt
thou do for a father?
Son
If he were dead, you'd weep for him; if you would not,
it were a good sign that I should quickly have a new   60
father.
Lady Macduff
Poor prattler, how thou talk'st!

145

63. Ross's warnings were vague, but this Messenger's are much more urgent. The pace of the scene changes abruptly.

64. *Though in your state ... perfect* Although I know your honourable status very well.

65. *I doubt* I am afraid.

66. *homely* humble.

70–71. 'It is cruel of me to frighten you in this way; to do worse to you would be monstrous'. He makes it plain in the next line that someone is likely to *do worse* to her soon.

73–5. *where to do harm ... folly* 'where doing harm often receives praise, and doing good is regarded as dangerous and stupid'. The complete reversal of values under Macbeth's tyranny is made clear.

81. *shag-ear'd* if this is the word Shakespeare actually wrote (which is doubtful) it probably means 'with hair sprouting from the ears' – the kind of thing a child might well notice.

81–2. *egg* and *fry* These are contemptuous terms applied to Lady Macduff's son because of his youthfulness and small stature.

[Enter a MESSENGER.*]*

Messenger
    Bless you, fair dame! I am not to you known,
    Though in your state of honour I am perfect.
    I doubt some danger does approach you nearly.   65
    If you will take a homely man's advice,
    Be not found here; hence, with your little ones.
    To fright you thus, methinks, I am too savage;
    To do worse to you were fell cruelty,
    Which is too nigh your person. Heaven preserve you   70
    I dare abide no longer.

[Exit.]

Lady Macduff
                    Whither should I fly?
    I have done no harm. But I remember now
    I am in this earthly world, where to do harm
    Is often laudable, to do good sometime
    Accounted dangerous folly. Why then, alas,   75
    Do I put up that unmanly defence
    To say I have done no harm?

[Enter MURDERERS.*]*

                    What are these faces?
First Murderer
    Where is your husband?
Lady Macduff
    I hope, in no place so unsanctified
    Where such as thou mayst find him.
First Murderer
                            He's a traitor.   80
Son
    Thou liest, thou shag-ear' d villain.
First Murderer
                            What, you egg?

82. *fry* baby fish.

[stabbing him]
Young fry of treachery!
Son

He has kill'd me, mother.
Run away, I pray you.

[Dies. Exit LADY MACDUFF, *crying 'Murder!'.]*

SCENE 3

Macbeth, the tyrant, now has a firm hold on Scotland. Malcolm, in the safety of the English court, naturally suspects anyone who comes from Scotland to persuade him to go back there, and he therefore tests Macduff's honesty.

1–2. Malcolm puts on a show of indicating that he has no hope and can only accept the situation passively. Macduff, on the other hand, urges active opposition to Macbeth.

3. *the mortal sword* the sword that kills.
4. *Bestride ... birthdom* defend our native country in its misfortune
5–8. *new sorrows ... dolour* woeful cries at fresh miseries are a blow (a 'slap in the face') to the forces of goodness. Heaven echoes with similar *(Like)* wails, in sympathy with Scotland.
8–17. Malcolm replies cautiously, almost as though he is saying; 'I regret any unhappiness that can be proved to have occurred, and I'll put right anything I can, if a suitable time *(time to friend)* comes.' Then he quite openly expresses his doubts about Macduff (lines 12–13); 'People once believed what Macbeth said – and you have shown respect and loyalty to him in the past. What's more, it's suspicious that he hasn't harmed you. I may seem gullible, but I can see that you might win favour with Macbeth by harming me. It might be in your interest to sacrifice a helpless creature (like me) to placate him.'

19–20. *A good ... charge* even a good man may falter and step back (into evil ways) when a king gives the orders.
21. *transpose* change. Malcolm means 'You are what you are; my suspicions of you won't make you vicious'.
22. *the brightest* Lucifer, who turned against God and was cast out.

Scene 3

England. Before King Edward's palace

[Enter MALCOLM and MACDUFF.]

Malcolm

    Let us seek out some desolate shade, and there
    Weep our sad bosoms empty.

Macduff

                    Let us rather
    Hold fast the mortal sword, and like good men
    Bestride our down-fall'n birthdom. Each new morn
    New widows howl, new orphans cry; new sorrows   5
    Strike heaven on the face, that it resounds
    As if it felt with Scotland and yell'd out
    Like syllable of dolour.

Malcolm

                What I believe, I'll wail;
    What know, believe: and what I can redress,
    As I shall find the time to friend, I will.   10
    What you have spoke, it may be so perchance.
    This tyrant, whose sole name blisters our tongues,
    Was once thought honest; you have lov'd him well;
    He hath not touch'd you yet. I am young; but
        something
    You may deserve of him through'me; and wisdom   15
    To offer up a weak, poor, innocent lamb
    T' appease an angry god.

Macduff

    I am not treacherous.

Malcolm

                But Macbeth is.
    A good and virtuous nature may recoil
    In an imperial charge. But I shall crave your pardon;   20
    That which you are, my thoughts cannot transpose;
    Angels are bright still, though the brightest fell.

25. The thought in Malcolm's mind seems to be that perhaps Macbeth promised Macduff that his family would be left unharmed if he betrayed Malcolm.

26. *rawness* unprotected state.

29–31. 'Don't let my suspicions alone dishonour you. I'm simply protecting myself by voicing them'. He ends, apologetically, by saying that Macduff may very well be an honest man, in spite of *these* suspicions.

33. *For goodness ... thee* Macduff bitterly accuses Malcolm of being too feeble to oppose Macbeth.

33–4. *Wear thou ... affeer'd* (the 'thou' here is Macbeth) go on enjoying the fruits of your crimes; you're undisputed master now.

34. *affeer'd* a legal term meaning 'confirmed'.

34. Macduff gives up the attempt and turns to go. But Malcolm has by no means completed his testing yet.

37. The Elizabethans thought of the East as the main source of gold and precious stones.

37. *to boot* as well.

39. *sinks beneath the yoke* The country is like an ill-treated animal pulling a heavy load.

41. *withal* moreover.

42. That people would support my cause.

43. *gracious England* King Edward the Confessor, who has God's grace.

44. From this point onwards Malcolm deliberately paints a frightful portrait of himself. He wants to see if Macduff would accept him as king, however evil he is; if so, then his suspicions will be proved to be correct – Macduff has come to trap him.

44. *for all this* in spite of all this.

Though all things foul would wear the brows of grace,
Yet grace must still look so.
Macduff

                       I have lost my hopes.
Malcolm

Perchance even there where I did find my doubts.   25
Why in that rawness left you wife and child,
Those precious motives, those strong knots of love,
Without leave-taking? I pray you,
Let not my jealousies be your dishonours,
But mine own safeties. You may be rightly just,   30
Whatever I shall think.
Macduff

                 Bleed, bleed, poor country.
Great tyranny, lay thou thy basis sure,
For goodness dare not check thee. Wear thou thy
       wrongs,
The title is affeer'd. Fare thee well, lord.
I would not be the villain that thou think'st   35
For the whole space that's in the tyrant's grasp
And the rich East to boot.
Malcolm

               Be not offended.
I speak not as in absolute fear of you.
I think our country sinks beneath the yoke;
It weeps, it bleeds; and each new day a gash   40
Is added to her wounds. I think withal
There would be hands uplifted in my right;
And here, from gracious England, have I offer
Of goodly thousands. But, for all this,
When I shall tread upon the tyrant's head,   45
Or wear it on my sword, yet my poor country
Shall have more vices than it had before;
More suffer, and more sundry ways than ever,
By him that shall succeed.
Macduff

              What should he be?

51. *particulars* detailed varieties.
51. *grafted* included, attached

54–5. *Esteem him ... harms* Think of Macbeth as being as innocent as a lamb, in contrast with my unlimited *(confineless)* vices.

58. *Luxurious* lustful.
58. *avaricious* miserly.
There is no evidence that Macbeth has either of these faults, but Malcolm is now presenting a kind of 'fantasy Macbeth', the sum of all evils, in order to declare himself even worse!
59. *Sudden* violent.
59. *smacking* tasting.
60–1. *but ... voluptuousness* my lustfulness has no limit.
63–5. *my desire ... my will* my lust would overcome all attempts to limit it.
66. We may imagine Macduff being silent for a few moments, not knowing what to say to such an astonishing piece of self-criticism. Then he admits that lustfulness has been the downfall of many rulers; nevertheless, even this may not rule Malcolm out as an improvement upon Macbeth as King of Scotland!
70–2. You may satisfy all your sexual desires lavishly in secret, preserving a reputation for self-control, by deceiving everyone.

73–6. That greedy creature, your lust, can't possibly take as many women as are willing to offer themselves to a king ...

76–84. Malcolm now moves on to the second major vice he accuses himself of – greed for possessions *(avarice)*.
77. *ill–compos'd affection* unbalanced character

Malcolm
It is myself I mean; in whom I know   50
All the particulars of vice so grafted
That, when they shall be open'd, black Macbeth
Will seem as pure as snow; and the poor state
Esteem him as a lamb, being compar'd
With my confineless harms.
Macduff
                                        Not in the legions   55
Of horrid hell can come a devil more damn'd
In evils to top Macbeth.
Malcolm
                                        I grant him bloody,
Luxurious, avaricious, false, deceitful,
Sudden, malicious, smacking of every sin
That has a name; but there's no bottom, none,   60
In my voluptuousness. Your wives, your daughters,
Your matrons, and your maids, could not fill up
The cistern of my lust; and my desire
All continent impediments would o'erbear
That did oppose my will. Better Macbeth   65
Than such an one to reign.
Macduff
                                        Boundless intemperance
In nature is a tyranny; it hath been
Th' untimely emptying of the happy throne
And fall of many kings. But fear not yet
To take upon you what is yours. You may   70
Convey your pleasures in a spacious plenty,
And yet seem cold, the tune you may so hoodwink.
We have willing dames enough; there cannot be
That vulture in you to devour so many
As will to greatness dedicate themselves,   75
Finding it so inclin'd.
Malcolm
                        With this there grows
In my most ill-compos'd affection such

78. *stanchless* uncontrollable.
79. *cut off* kill.
80. *his* one nobleman's.

82–3. *that I should ... unjust* make up false complaints (as excuses for robbing them).

86–9. *summer-seeming* Macduff's point is that lust isn't likely to last throughout a man's life (it will pass, like summer), but avarice is different, and worse. Even so, Scotland can probably cope with this, too.
88. *foisons* plentiful resources.
89. *Of your mere own* out of what really belongs to you (as king).
89. *portable* bearable.
92. *verity*: truthfulness.
93. *Bounty* generosity.

95. *I have no relish of them* I haven't a scrap of any of these in me.
96. In variations of every possible sin.

97–100. This is just the kind of conclusive, all-embracingly destructive threat that Macbeth makes at his most desperate moments (see Act 4, Scene 1, lines 57–60). Malcolm still seems to be using the tyrant as his model of wickedness.
98. *concord* harmony.
99. *Uproar* throw into chaos.

102. Macduff has now had enough, and gives up his attempt to persuade Malcolm.
104. *untitled* not entitled to the throne.

A stanchless avarice that, were I King,
I should cut off the nobles for their lands,
Desire his jewels, and this other's house;   80
And my more-having would be as a sauce
To make me hunger more, that I should forge
Quarrels unjust against the good and loyal,
Destroying them for wealth.
Macduff
       This avarice
Sticks deeper, grows with more pernicious root   85
Than summer-seeming lust; and it hath been
The sword of our slain kings. Yet do not fear;
Scotland hath foisons to fill up your will
Of your mere own. All these are portable,
With other graces weigh'd.   90
Malcolm
But I have none. The king-becoming graces,
As justice, verity, temp'rance, stableness,
Bounty, perseverance, mercy, lowliness,
Devotion, patience, courage, fortitude,
I have no relish of them; but abound   95
In the division of each several crime,
Acting it many ways. Nay, had I pow'r, I should
Pour the sweet milk of concord into hell,
Uproar the universal peace, confound
All unity on earth.
Macduff
      O Scotland, Scotland!   100
Malcolm
If such a one be fit to govern, speak.
I am as I have spoken.
Macduff
     Fit to govern!
No, not to live! O nation miserable,
With an untitled tyrant bloody-scept'red,
When shalt thou see thy wholesome days again,   105
Since that the truest issue of thy throne

107. *interdiction* condemnation.

108. *blaspheme his breed* disgrace his family.

111. *Died every day she liv'd* she was so devout that she lived every day as if it were her last.

112–13. *These evils ... Hath* we now regard *Hath* as a singular verb, but it was often used with a plural subject in Shakespeare's time.

113. *breast* heart (thought to be the source of feelings).

115. *Child of integrity* i.e. 'which was inspired by your honest nature'. Malcolm is now satisfied that Macduff is not acting a sinister part.

116. *black scruples* dark suspicions.

118. *trains* tricks, schemes.

119–20. *and modest wisdom ... haste* commonsense has prevented me from believing things too easily.

120–1. Malcolm's appeal to God's grace, putting fears and doubts away in the process, sets the tone for the remainder of the play, as the forces of good seek to overthrow the forces of evil represented by Macbeth.

123. *Unspeak mine own detraction* take back the things I accused myself of.

123. *abjure* deny.

125. *For strangers ... nature* as qualities quite foreign to me.

126. *Unknown to woman* virginal.

126. *never was forsworn* never dishonoured by being false.

127. Far from wanting things, Malcolm declares he doesn't particularly value his own possessions, let alone those of others.

135. *at a point* fully prepared for action.

136–7. *the chance of goodness ... quarrel!* may our chances of success be as great as the justice of our cause'

138–9. It is not hard to sympathize with Macduff's bewilderment. But could Malcolm have tested him in any more effective way?

By his own interdiction stands accurs'd
And does blaspheme his breed? Thy royal father
Was a most sainted king; the queen that bore thee,
Oft'ner upon her knees than on her feet,   110
Died every day she liv'd. Fare thee well!
These evils thou repeat'st upon thyself
Hath banish'd me from Scotland. O my breast,
Thy hope ends here!
Malcolm

                  Macduff, this noble passion,
Child of integrity, hath from my soul   115
Wip'd the black scruples, reconcil'd my thoughts
To thy good truth and honour. Devilish Macbeth
By many of these trains hath sought to win me
Into his power; and modest wisdom plucks me
From over-credulous haste. But God above   120
Deal between thee and me; for even now
I put myself to thy direction, and
Unspeak mine own detraction, here abjure
The taints and blames I laid upon myself
For strangers to my nature. I am yet   125
Unknown to woman, never was forsworn,
Scarcely have coveted what was mine own,
At no time broke my faith, would not betray
The devil to his fellow, and delight
No less in truth than life. My first false speaking   130
Was this upon myself. What I am truly
Is thine and my poor country's to command:
Whither indeed, before thy here-approach,
Old Siward with ten thousand warlike men
Already at a point was setting forth.   135
Now we'll together; and the chance of goodness
Be like our warranted quarrel! Why are you silent?
Macduff
Such welcome and unwelcome things at once
'Tis hard to reconcile.

140–59. In this passage Edward the Confessor (the King of England) is presented as a source of healing. Not only can he heal the glandular disease, scrofula (the tradition that English sovereigns possessed this power continued until at least Queen Anne's time), but it is also implied that he can heal political and social evils, like Macbeth's regime. It is the support of Edward's soldiers that make it possible for Malcolm to return powerfully to Scotland.

142. *stay his cure* wait for him to cure them.

142–3. *Convinces ... art* defeats all the skill of trained doctors.

145. *presently amend* immediately get better.

146. Scrofula is often called 'the King's Evil'.

149. *solicits heaven* secures help from God.

150. *strangely-visited* horribly afflicted.

152. *mere* sheer.

153. *stamp* coin.

155–6. His successors on the throne will inherit his blessed healing power.

160. Apparently Malcolm sees that Ross is wearing Scottish clothes, but does not at first recognize him, although we know they have met before (see Act 1, Scene 6). Perhaps he is again suspicious of a visitor from Scotland, until Macduff greets him warmly.

[Enter a DOCTOR.*]*

Malcolm

Well; more anon. Comes the King forth, I pray you?   140

Doctor

Ay, sir. There are a crew of wretched souls
That stay his cure. Their malady convinces
The great assay of art; but at his touch,
Such sanctity hath heaven given his hand,
They presently amend.

Malcolm

I thank you, doctor.   145

[Exit DOCTOR.*]*

Macduff

What's the disease he means?

Malcolm

'Tis called the evil:
A most miraculous work in this good king,
Which often since my hero-remain in England
I have seen him do. How he solicits heaven,
Himself best knows; but strangely-visited people,   150
All swoln and ulcerous, pitiful to the eye,
The mere despair of surgery, he cures,
Hanging a golden stamp about their necks,
Put on with holy prayers; and 'tis spoken,
To the succeeding royalty he leaves   155
The healing benediction. With this strange virtue,
He hath a heavenly gift of prophecy;
And sundry blessings hang about his throne
That speak him full of grace.

[Enter ROSS.*]*

Macduff

See, who comes here?

Malcolm

My countryman; but yet I know him not.   160

162. *betimes* quickly.
163. The things (such as a foul dictatorship) which make men suspicious of each other.

166–7. *nothing … knows nothing* no one except the *most* ignorant person (e.g. an imbecile).
168. *rent* rend.
169. *Are made, not mark'd* uttered, but not noticed (because agonized cries are so common).
170. *A modern ecstasy* a familiar emotion, something like 'a fashionable disease'.
170–1. *the dead man's knell … for who* people hardly bother to ask who's dead when they hear the bell tolling.
173. 'Dying before they fall ill' – probably because so many are being 'liquidated' by Macbeth's agents.
173–4. *O, relation … true!* Your account is too full of horrid detail, but undeniably true.

175. Any news an hour old earns the teller hisses (because it's stale. Evil things are happening all the time).
176. *teems* gives birth to.
176–240. In the rest of the scene Ross finds it difficult to break the news of the slaughter of Macduff's family, and when he does so Macduff is at first almost struck dumb with horror. Only when he expresses his feelings of sorrow and anger can he cope with the dreadful event. Then he is ready to seek a righteous revenge.

Macduff
 My ever gentle cousin, welcome hither.
Malcolm
 I know him now. Good God betimes remove
 The means that makes us strangers!
Ross
         Sir, amen.
Macduff
 Stands Scotland where it did?
Ross
        Alas, poor country,
 Almost afraid to know itself! It cannot   165
 Be call'd our mother, but our grave; where nothing,
 But who knows nothing, is once seen to smile;
 Where sighs, and groans, and shrieks, that rent the air,
 Are made, not mark'd; where violent sorrow seems
 A modern ecstasy; the dead man's knell   170
 Is there scarce ask'd for who; and good men's lives
 Expire before the flowers in their caps,
 Dying or ere they sicken.
Macduff
       O, relation
 Too nice, and yet too true!
Malcolm
        What's the newest grief?
Ross
 That of an hour's age doth hiss the speaker: 175
 Each minute teems a new one.
Macduff
       How does my wife?
Ross
 Why, well.
Macduff
    And all my children?
Ross
        Well too.

179. *well at peace* It seems cruel to use a pun at such a time; but it does convey Ross's uneasiness and unwillingness to lie or reveal the dreadful news.

180. *a niggard of your speech* so reluctant to speak.

181–3. *the tidings* probably the news of the death of Lady Macduff and her children which he is yet to reveal.

183. *were out* had left their homes to oppose Macbeth.

185. *the tyrant's power afoot* Macbeth's army mobilized.

186. *your eye ...* Ross has turned from Macduff, only too glad to avoid conversation with him, and is addressing Malcolm.

188. *To doff ... distresses* To get rid of their troubles, as though throwing off clothes.

189. Exactly the same phrase was used of King Edward in line 43.

191. *older* more experienced.

192. *gives out* proclaims.

195. *Where hearing ... them* Where they wouldn't be heard by anyone.

195. *latch* catch.

196–7. *a fee-grief ... breast?* a sorrow belonging to one particular person.

197–8. *No mind ... some woe* All decent people feel sympathy for those who suffer, and thus suffer themselves.

199. *pertains* relates

Macduff
The tyrant has not batter'd at their peace?
Ross
No; they were well at peace when I did leave 'em.
Macduff
Be not a niggard of your speech. How goes't?   180
Ross
When I came hither to transport the tidings,
Which I have heavily borne, there ran a rumour
Of many worthy fellows that were out;
Which was to my belief witnessed the rather
For that I saw the tyrant's power afoot.   185
Now is the time of help; your eye in Scotland
Would create soldiers, make our women fight,
To doff their dire distresses.
Malcolm
                                        Be't their comfort
We are coming thither. Gracious England hath
Lent us good Siward and ten thousand men –   190
An older and a better soldier none
That Christendom gives out.
Ross
                                        Would I could answer
This comfort with the like! But I have words
That would be howl'd out in the desert air,
Where hearing should not latch them.
Macduff
                                        What concern they?   195
The general cause, or is it a fee-grief
Due to some single breast?
Ross
                                        No mind that's honest
But in it shares some woe, though the main part
Pertains to you alone.
Macduff
                                        If it be mine.
Keep it not from me; quickly let me have it.   200

202. *possess them* inform them.

205–7. *To relate … death of you* To tell you in detail how it happened would add your death to the deaths of those you loved.
206. *quarry* means a heap of animals killed in hunting, and *deer* is a deeply sympathetic pun on 'dear'.

208–9. Macduff has tried not to show his feelings to the others, by hiding his face. Malcolm knows that he must express what he feels *(Give sorrow words…).*
210. *o'erfraught* overburdened.

212. *And I must … thence!* And I had to be absent at the time!

216. *He has no children* There are several possible explanations of this remark, the most likely being that it is addressed to Macbeth and means that Macduff cannot take an appropriate revenge ('tit for tat'). It might, alternatively, be addressed to Ross or himself and refer to Malcolm who doesn't yet know what it is to have a father's feelings.
217. *hell–kite* a devilish bird of prey, raiding a chicken-run and killing all the birds.
218. *dam* mother.

Ross
    Let not your ears despise my tongue for ever,
    Which shall possess them with the heaviest sound
    That ever yet they heard.
Macduff
                    Hum! I guess at it.
Ross
    Your castle is surpris'd; your wife and babes
    Savagely slaughter'd. To relate the manner,   205
    Were, on the quarry of these murder'd deer,
    To add the death of you.
Malcolm
                  Merciful heaven!
    What, man! Ne'er pull your hat upon your brows;
    Give sorrow words. The grief that does not speak
    Whispers the o'erfraught heart and bids it break.   210
Macduff
    My children too?
Ross
             Wife, children, servants, all
    That could be found.
Macduff
              And I must be from thence!
    My wife kill'd too?
Ross
           I have said.
Malcolm
                Be comforted.
    Let's make us med'cines of our great revenge
    To cure this deadly grief.   215
Macduff
    He has no children. All my pretty ones?
    Did you say all? O hell-kite! All?
    What, all my pretty chickens and their dam
    At one fell swoop?
Malcolm
    Dispute it like a man.

222. *things* beings (i.e. Lady Macduff and the children).

225. *nought* evil.

226–7. *Not for their own ... souls* 'They died because of my sinfulness, not their own'. Macduff sees their deaths as the consequence of his own sins, but he is probably not blaming himself for having left his family in Scotland – that was an unfortunate necessity.

228. *whetstone* a piece of stone on which knives (and swords) are sharpened.

229. *blunt not ... it* don't tone down your feelings; express them in full force.

230–1. Macduff declares that he could easily act like a woman (by weeping) or like a boaster (by merely saying what he will do); instead, he intends to return to Scotland and get his revenge.

232. *Cut short all intermission* cut out all delay.

232. *front to front* face to face.

235. *Heaven forgive him too!* He means that if Macbeth escapes with his life it will mean that he, Macduff, has first forgiven him.

235. *This tune goes manly* This is a proper, manly way of speaking.

237. *Our lack ... leave* The only thing left to do is to say our farewells.

237–9. *Macbeth ... their instruments* Macbeth is compared to a ripe fruit which is ready to fall.

238–9. *the pow'rs above ... instruments* he means that God has selected them as the agents of divine vengeance.

240. He implies that dawn (which will bring light and therefore hope) will soon break and that the fortunes of all good, true people in Scottish society are about to change.

Macduff

                        I shall do so;   220
But I must also feel it as a man.
I cannot but remember such things were
That were most precious to me. Did heaven look on,
And would not take their part? Sinful Macduff,
They were all struck for thee – nought that I am;   225
Not for their own demerits, but for mine,
Fell slaughter on their souls. Heaven rest them now!

Malcolm

Be this the whetstone of your sword. Let grief
Convert to anger; blunt not the heart, enrage it.

Macduff

O, I could play the woman with mine eyes   230
And braggart with my tongue! But, gentle heavens,
Cut short all intermission; front to front
Bring thou this fiend of Scotland and myself;
Within my sword's length set him; if he scape,
Heaven forgive him too!

Malcolm

                    This tune goes manly.   235
Come, go we to the King. Our power is ready;
Our lack is nothing but our leave. Macbeth
Is ripe for shaking, and the pow'rs above
Put on their instruments. Receive what cheer you may;
The night is long that never finds the day.   240

[Exeunt.]

ACT 5 SCENE 1

We have not seen Lady Macbeth since the middle of Act 3. At that point (Scene 4) she was still trying to comfort and strengthen her husband (*You lack the season of all natures, sleep* were her last words then), but he was beginning to act alone, without communication with her. Now it is she who cannot sleep and who lives in a dreadful world of guilty visions. The scene is introduced almost like a documentary by the Doctor and the Gentlewoman, preparing the way for Lady Macbeth's wild but significant remarks.

1. *watch'd* stayed up at night to watch.

3. *went into the field* led his army against the rebels.

5. *closet* a writing-cabinet. What do you imagine Lady Macbeth wrote?

8–9. *A great perturbation ... watching!* A terrible disorder, to be asleep yet at the same time to act as though awake!
11. *actual performances* actions.

14. *meet* correct, fitting.
15–16. The Gentlewoman has more sense, in Macbeth's Scotland, with secret agents everywhere, than to say anything which can't be conclusively proved.

17. *This is her very guise* This is exactly as she looked before.
18. *stand close* stay hidden.

ACT 5

Scene 1

Dunsinane. Macbeth's castle

[Enter a DOCTOR OF PHYSIC *and a* WAITING-GENTLEWOMAN.*]*

Doctor

I have two nights watch'd with you, but can perceive
no truth in your report. When was it she last walk'd?

Gentlewoman

Since his Majesty went into the field, I have seen her
rise from her bed, throw her nightgown upon her,
unlock her closet, take forth paper, fold it, write   5
upon't, read it, afterwards seal it, and again return to
bed; yet all this while in a most fast sleep.

Doctor

A great perturbation in nature, to receive at once the
benefit of sleep and do the effects of watching! In this
slumb'ry agitation, besides her walking and other   10
actual performances, what, at any time, have you
heard her say?

Gentlewoman

That, sir, which I will not report after her.

Doctor

You may to me; and 'tis most meet you should.

Gentlewoman

Neither to you nor any one, having no witness to   15
confirm my speech.

[Enter LADY MACBETH, *with a taper.]*

Lo you, here she comes! This is her very guise; and,
upon my life, fast asleep. Observe her; stand close.

Doctor

How came she by that light?

20–1. There is a horrible irony in the fact that the woman who said *Come, thick night. And pall thee in the dunnest smoke of hell* (Act 1, Scene 5, lines 50–1) should now be, like a nervous child, afraid of the dark. On the other hand it might be said that she herself is now *in the dunnest smoke of hell.*

24–8. She stops at this point, puts down the candle, and stands desperately going through the motions of washing—an *accustomed action* since her 'nervous breakdown'.

29. *Yet* still, even now.

29. *a spot* of blood (though she had told her husband *A little water clears us of this deed.* Act 2, Scene 2, line 67).

31. *satisfy my remembrance* back up and confirm what I remember later.

32. *One, two* either the bell she struck as a signal for Macbeth (Act 2, Scene 1, lines 31–2) or, more likely, the clock striking in the night when Duncan was murdered.

33. *Hell is murky* i.e. the hell she is now in. Her broken speeches are a mix of her past, cold comments when she encouraged Macbeth to act, and horrified remarks which show the more sensitive womanly nature she deliberately repressed. Do you think we are getting a more accurate picture of her as a person now than when we watched her behaving like a monster before?

39. *The Thane of Fife* … now? What effect does the 'nursery rhyme' have?

41–2. *you mar all with this starting* She recalls her anger and dismay when Macbeth broke down at the banquet, and said he saw Banquo's ghost.

43. *Go to, go to* The Doctor can't resist expressing his deep concern about the deeds her words hint at.

Gentlewoman

Why, it stood by her. She has light by her continually;   20
'tis her command.

Doctor

You see her eyes are open.

Gentlewoman

Ay, but their sense is shut.

Doctor

What is it she does now? Look how she rubs her
hands.   25

Gentlewoman

It is an accustomed action with her, to seem thus
washing her hands; I have known her continue in
this a quarter of an hour.

Lady Macbeth

Yet here's a spot.

Doctor

Hark, she speaks. I will set down what comes from   30
her, to satisfy my remembrance the more strongly.

Lady Macbeth

Out, damned spot! Out, I say! One, two; why then
'tis time to do't. Hell is murky. Fie, my lord, fie! a
soldier, and afeard? What need we fear who knows
it, when none can call our pow'r to account? Yet who   35
would have thought the old man to have had so
much blood in him?

Doctor

Do you mark that?

Lady Macbeth

The Thane of Fife had a wife; where is she now?
What, will these hands ne'er be clean? No more o'   40
that, my lord, no more o' that; you mar all with this
starting.

Doctor

Go to, go to; you have known what you should not.

Gentlewoman

She has spoke what she should not, I am sure of that.

173

46–7. *All the perfumes ... hand* a close parallel with the similar hopelessness of Macbeth's ***Will all great Neptune's ocean wash this blood Clean from my hand?*** (Act 2, Scene 2, lines 60–1.)

50. *dignity* value, rank or position.
51–2. Even in such a small part as the Gentlewoman's, we notice she has a talent for shrewd and sharp comment.

53. *my practice* my medical expertise.

58. *out on's grave* out of his grave.

61–2. *What's done cannot be undone* There is, again, deep irony in such shoulder-shrugging words coming from a woman broken by the deeds she dismisses.

65. *Foul whisperings are abroad* evil rumours are going around.
65–6. *Unnatural deeds ... troubles* the unnatural deeds of leaders like Macbeth lead to unnatural events like rebellion (anything which breaks public order being, in a sense, unnatural).

Heaven knows what she has known. 45

Lady Macbeth
Here's the smell of the blood still. All the perfumes
of Arabia will not sweeten this little hand. Oh, oh,
oh!

Doctor
What a sigh is there! The heart is sorely charg'd.

Gentlewoman
I would not have such a heart in my bosom for the
dignity of the whole body. 50

Doctor
Well, well, well.

Gentlewoman
Pray God it be, sir.

Doctor
This disease is beyond my practice. Yet I have known
those which have walk'd in their sleep who have
died holily in their beds. 55

Lady Macbeth
Wash your hands, put on your nightgown, look not
so pale. I tell you yet again, Banquo's buried; he cannot come out on's grave.

Doctor
Even so?

Lady Macbeth
To bed, to bed; there's knocking at the gate. Come, 60
come, come, come, give me your hand. What's done
cannot be undone. To bed, to bed, to bed.

[Exit.]

Doctor
Will she go now to bed?

Gentlewoman
Directly.

Doctor
Foul whisp'rings are abroad. Unnatural deeds 65

66. *infected minds* diseased or corrupted minds, like Lady Macbeth's.

68. She needs a priest to save her soul, rather than a doctor to heal her body.

70. *means of all annoyance* all means of injuring herself (in particular, of committing suicide).

71. *still* always, constantly.

72. *mated* bewildered.

Do breed unnatural troubles; infected minds
To their deaf pillows will discharge their secrets.
More needs she the divine than the physician.
God, God forgive us all. Look after her;
Remove from her the means of all annoyance,   70
And still keep eyes upon her. So, good night.
My mind she has mated, and amaz'd my sight.
I think, but dare not speak. Gentlewoman
Good night, good doctor.

[Exeunt.]

SCENE 2

The purpose of this short scene is to show that there are other Scotsmen who are prepared to work tirelessly to rid their country of tyranny. Malcolm and Macduff can expect considerable assistance from inside their own country, as well as from outside.

3–5. *for their dear causes ... man* for their heartfelt causes would bring to life even a dead man to fight the bloody battle.
6. *Shall we well meet them* we are likely to meet them.

8. *file* list.
10. *unrough* smooth-cheeked (too young to shave yet).

11. *Protest ... manhood* insist on showing (by fighting) that they are now men.

15–16. *He cannot buckle ... rule* 'He can no longer impose his will on a failing situation' (the image is of a plump man – perhaps swollen with dropsy – trying to control his waistline.)
17. *sticking on his hands* i.e. the blood shed in the murders.
18–20. *Now minutely ... love* Minute by minute men desert him, reflecting and condemning his own treachery (when he betrayed his king). Those who remain faithful on the surface obey him only because they are under orders, not because they love him.
20–2. *Now does ... thief.* He has put on royal robes, but he lacks the royal nature to fill them.

Scene 2

The country near Dunsinane

[Drum and colours. Enter MENTEITH, CAITHNESS, ANGUS,
LENNOX *and* SOLDIERS.*]*

Menteith

    The English pow'r is near, led on by Malcolm,
    His uncle Siward, and the good Macduff.
    Revenges burn in them; for their dear causes
    Would to the bleeding and the grim alarm
    Excite the mortified man.

Angus

                    Near Birnam wood   5
    Shall we well meet them; that way are they coming.

Caithness

    Who knows if Donalbain be with his brother?

Lennox

    For certain, sir, he is not; I have a file
    Of all the gentry. There is Siward's son,
    And many unrough youths that even now   10
    Protest their first of manhood.

Menteith

                What does the tyrant?

Caithness

    Great Dunsinane he strongly fortifies.
    Some say he's mad; others, that lesser hate him,
    Do call it valiant fury; but for certain
    He cannot buckle his distempered cause   15
    Within the belt of rule.

Angus

             Now does he feel
    His secret murders sticking on his hands;
    Now minutely revolts upbraid his faith-breach;
    Those he commands move only in command,
    Nothing in love. Now does he feel his title   20

22–5. *Who then ... being there?* Who could blame Macbeth's own troubled senses for reacting violently when they condemn themselves for belonging to him..

27. *med'cine* probably, as in French, 'doctor'– referring to Malcolm, who has come to heal the state *(sickly weal).*

28–9. They will shed their blood, which is Scottish, in order to cure Scotland of its disease. (Bleeding was an important form of treatment for many illnesses.)

30. To make Malcolm's cause flourish and to destroy Macbeth and those who support him.

Hang loose about him, like a giant's robe
Upon a dwarfish thief.
Menteith
                   Who then shall blame
His pester'd senses to recoil and start,
When all that is within him does condemn
Itself for being there?
Caithness
                Well, march we on   25
To give obedience where 'tis truly ow'd.
Meet we the med'cine of the sickly weal;
And with him pour we in our country's purge
Each drop of us.
Lennox
             Or so much as it needs
To dew the sovereign flower and drown the weeds.   30
Make we our march towards Birnam.

    [Exeunt, marching.]

SCENE 3

Macbeth drives himself on by referring to the witches' most recent prophecies, but he is increasingly desperate and has little else to encourage him: his wife is mentally unstable, he has no real friends, and his castle is being hemmed in by the English forces under Malcolm, Siward and Macduff, and by those Scots who have already rebelled.

1. *let them fly all* (I don't care) if all my thanes leave me.
3. *taint with fear* be weakened by the disease of fear.

4–5. *The spirits ... consequences* The witches who know everything that is going to happen to human beings.

8. *epicures* luxury-loving people: the tough Scots perhaps tended to look on the English as pampered Southerners.
9. *sway by* rule myself with.

11–19. The number of times Macbeth refers to the messenger's (not surprising) paleness is quite astonishing, *cream-fac'd, goose look, prick thy face, and over-red thy fear, lily-liver'd,* possibly *patch* (which can mean 'plaster' as well as 'fool' or 'clown'), *linen cheeks,* and *whey-face.* Such crazy repetition may suggest Macbeth's obsessive nature.
11. *loon* rogue.

17. *Are counsellors to fear* make other people afraid.
17. *whey-face* a fellow with a face the colour of skimmed milk.

Scene 3

Dunsinane. Macbeth's castle

[Enter MACBETH, DOCTOR *and* ATTENDANTS.*]*

Macbeth
　Bring me no more reports; let them fly all.
　Till Birnam wood remove to Dunsinane
　I cannot taint with fear. What's the boy Malcolm?
　Was he not born of woman? The spirits that know
　All mortal consequences have pronounc'd me thus:　　5
　'Fear not, Macbeth; no man that's born of woman
　Shall e'er have power upon thee'. Then fly, false thane
　And mingle with the English epicures.
　The mind I sway by and the heart I bear
　Shall never sag with doubt nor shake with fear.　　10

[Enter SERVANT.*]*

　The devil damn thee black, thou cream-fac'd loon!
　Where got'st thou that goose look?

Servant
　There is ten thousand –
Macbeth
　　　　　　　　Geese, villain?
Servant
　　　　　　　　　　　　Soldiers, sir.
Macbeth
　Go, prick thy face, and over-red thy fear,
　Thou lily-liver'd boy. What soldiers, patch?　　15
　Death of thy soul! Those linen cheeks of thine
　Are counsellors to fear. What soldiers, whey-face?
Servant
　The English force, so please you.
Macbeth
　Take thy face hence

20. *push* attack.

21. *disseat* remove from the throne.

22–8. It is some time since we have felt sympathy for Macbeth, but we might admire here his remarkable clear-sightedness when analysing himself and his life.

23. *Is fall'n ... leaf* Has come to autumn, the time of withered, yellow leaves.

23–6. Macbeth cannot hope to have any of the compensations of old age enjoyed by most reasonably happy men.

27. *mouth-honour* i.e. respectful words spoken but not meant. *breath* This conveys the same idea.

28. *Which the poor ... dare not* Which the faint-hearted speaker would like to hold back.

31. Presumably the arrival of the English army, and its size.

35. *moe* more.

35. *skirr* scour.

37. There is no real need for the doctor to come on until now, and in some productions this is how it is arranged.

[Exit SERVANT.*]*

        Seyton! – I am sick at heart,
When I behold – Seyton, I say! – This push   20
Will cheer me ever, or disseat me now.
I have liv'd long enough. My way of life
Is fall'n into the sear, the yellow leaf;
And that which should accompany old age,
As honour, love, obedience, troops of friends,   25
I must not look to have; but, in their stead,
Curses not loud but deep, mouth-honour, breath,
Which the poor heart would fain deny, and dare not.
Seyton!

[Enter SEYTON.*]*

Seyton
   What's your gracious pleasure?
Macbeth
                    What news more?   30
Seyton
   All is confirm'd, my lord, which was reported.
Macbeth
   I'll fight till from my bones my flesh be hack'd.
   Give me my armour.
Seyton
          'Tis not needed yet.
Macbeth
   I'd put it on.
   Send out more horses, skirr the country round;   35
   Hang those that talk of fear. Give me mine armour.
   How does your patient, doctor?
Doctor
             Not so sick, my lord,
As she is troubled with thick-coming fancies
That keep her from her rest.
Macbeth
             Cure her of that.

40–5. What Macbeth suggests that his wife needs is the skill of a modern psychiatrist, but certainly not of a medieval doctor.

42. *Raze out* erase.

43. *oblivious antidote* a medicine that will make the patient forget.

44. *stuff'd* overloaded.

47. *physic* the art of the doctor.

48. *staff* the symbol of his rank as commander-in-chief (the equivalent of a modern Field-Marshal's baton).

49. *Doctor … from me* What has this to do with the doctor?

50. *Come, sir, dispatch* 'Hurry up and get on with it' (addressed to Seyton).

50–1. *Cast … disease* diagnose the disease by examining the patient's urine. But the patient now is Scotland; Lady Macbeth has passed from his mind.

52. *pristine health* the health the country once enjoyed.
pristine former.

53–4. *I would applaud … again* I would applaud you so enthusiastically that the echoes would then applaud you too.

54. *Pull't off, I say* Macbeth seems to have changed his mind, and now tells Seyton to take his armour off again.

55. *rhubarb, senna, purgative drugs …* These are all laxatives. Macbeth wants something to purge the body of Scotland of the English intruders.

58. *it* his armour, or a piece of it.

59. *bane* destruction.

61. Probably both 'safe' ('in the clear') and 'unstained by evil'.

Canst thou not minister to a mind diseas'd,   40
Pluck from the memory a rooted sorrow,
Raze out the written troubles of the brain,
And with some sweet oblivious antidote
Cleanse the stuff'd bosom of that perilous stuff
Which weighs upon the heart?

Doctor

                          Therein the patient   45
Must minister to himself.

Macbeth

Throw physic to the dogs – I'll none of it.
Come, put mine armour on; give me my staff.
Seyton, send out. Doctor, the thanes fly from me.
Come, sir, dispatch. If thou couldst, doctor, cast   50
The water of my land, find her disease,
And purge it to a sound and pristine health,
I would applaud thee to the very echo,
That should applaud again.—Pull't off, I say. –
What rhubarb, senna, or what purgative drug,   55
Would scour these English hence? Hear'st thou of
        them?

Doctor

Ay, my good lord. Your royal preparation
Makes us hear something.

Macbeth

                    Bring it after me.
I will not be afraid of death and bane
Till Birnam Forest come to Dunsinane.   60

[Exeunt all but the DOCTOR.*]*

Doctor

Were I from Dunsinane away and clear,
Profit again should hardly draw me here.

[Exit.]

SCENE 4

The combined Scottish and English forces are now marching towards Dunsinane and are near Birnam Wood.

Stage Direction *colours* flags.

2. *That chambers will be safe* i.e. when people can sleep safely in their bedrooms again (unlike Duncan).
doubt it nothing have no doubt that it will be so.

5. *shadow* hide.
6. *host* army.
6–7. *make discovery ... of us* cause the enemy's scouts to make false reports about us.

8–10. *We learn. ... before't* All reports agree that the confident Macbeth stays all the time in the castle of Dunsinane and will allow us to besiege it (without leaving the castle to oppose us).

10. *'Tis his main hope* i.e. to 'sit tight', defending his castle.
11–12. For whenever any opportunity has presented itself, both high and low-ranking soldiers have deserted him.
13. *constrained things* wretched creatures forced to obey him.
14–16. *Let our just censures ... soldiership* Let us delay giving our opinions until we see how things turn out. In the meantime let's do our jobs as efficient soldiers.

Scene 4

Before Birnam Wood

[Drum and colours. Enter MALCOLM, SIWARD, MACDUFF,
SIWARD'S SON, MENTEITH, CAITHNESS, ANGUS, LENNOX,
ROSS *and* SOLDIERS, *marching.]*

Malcolm
  Cousins, I hope the days are near at hand
  That chambers will be safe.
Menteith
                  We doubt it nothing.
Siward
  What wood is this before us?
Menteith
                The wood of Birnam.
Malcolm
  Let every soldier hew him down a bough
  And bear't before him; thereby shall we shadow   5
  The numbers of our host, and make discovery
  Err in report of us.
Soldiers
          It shall be done.
Siward
  We learn no other but the confident tyrant
  Keeps still in Dunsinane, and will endure
  Our setting down before't.
Malcolm
            'Tis his main hope;   10
  For where there is advantage to be given,
  Both more and less have given him the revolt;
  And none serve with him but constrained things
  Whose hearts are absent too.
Macduff
           Let our just censures
  Attend the true event, and put we on   15

189

16–18. *The time approaches ... we owe* Soon, when fate has decided the event, we shall be able to separate our hopes (*What we shall say we have*) and our actual achievements *(what we owe).*

19–20. Talking can only raise fragile hopes. Fighting *(strokes)* is the way to decide the issue beyond doubt.

Industrious soldiership.
Siward.
                    The time approaches
That will with due decision make us know
What we shall say we have, and what we owe.
Thoughts speculative their unsure hopes relate,
But certain issue strokes must arbitrate;   20
Towards which advance the war.

        [Exeunt, marching.]

SCENE 5

Macbeth does at first seem the *confident tyrant* that Siward called him. It appears that he has overcome his old concerns and is now tough and indifferent to what happens to him. Is this impression confirmed as the scene goes on, or are there deeper, different emotions we begin to see?

3. *let them lie* let the besieging forces stay.
4. *ague* fever (infectious fevers of several kinds were very common in armies in those days).
5. *forc'd* reinforced.
5. *those that should be ours* Macbeth's way of referring to the *more and less who have given him the revolt.*
6. *dareful* defiantly.
6. *beard to beard* face to face.

10–13. *The time has been ... were in't* 'Formerly I would have shivered with fear at a cry in the night, and the hair would have stood up on my scalp as though it had a life of its own, when I heard a horrifying story.'
11. *fell* any skin with fur or hair on it.
14–15. *Direness ... start me* Horror, which has become a common part of my murderous thoughts, has no power now to startle me.

Scene 5

Dunsinane. Macbeth's castle

[Enter MACBETH, SEYTON and SOLDIERS, with drum and colours.]

Macbeth

Hang out our banners on the outward walls;
The cry is still 'They come'. Our castle's strength
Will laugh a siege to scorn. Here let them lie
Till famine and the ague eat them up.
Were they not forc'd with those that should be ours,   5
We might have met them dareful, beard to beard,
And beat them backward home.

[A cry within of women.]

                        What is that noise?

Seyton

It is the cry of women, my good lord.

[Exit]

Macbeth

I have almost forgot the taste of fears.
The time has been my senses would have cool'd   10
To hear a night-shriek, and my fell of hair
Would at a dismal treatise rouse and stir
As life were in't. I have supp'd full with horrors;
Direness, familiar to my slaughterous thoughts,
Cannot once start me.

[Re-enter SEYTON.]

                    Wherefore was that cry?   15

Seyton

The Queen, my lord, is dead.

17–28. Although he seemed concerned about his wife's health in Scene 3, his reaction to her death is strangely emotionless, yet it leads to a beautifully simple speech about the futility of life.

17–18. It would have been better if she had died later on, at a more convenient time for such news.

19. Notice how well this line puts across the plodding monotony of dreary days succeeding each other in a meaningless life.

21. *To the last syllable ... time* i.e. until the very last word of human history is written.

22–3. *And all ... death* And every day in the past stupid human beings have been able to see just well enough to move to their deaths and crumble to dust in their graves.

23. *Out, out, brief candle!* Macbeth's farewell to his wife.

24–6. *walking shadow* and *poor player* both are ways of referring to an actor. Shakespeare often refers to acting in a way which stresses its unreality and how it is impossible to present life meaningfully on the stage.

25. *struts and frets* the activity is hectic, but in no way significant.

26–8. *it is a tale ... nothing* a statement of extreme despair.

29. Do you think there should be a long pause after Macbeth's last words?

30. *Gracious my lord* 'My gracious lord.' Although there is no sign of grace in Macbeth now he is still the king and must be addressed in an appropriate manner.

39. *next* nearest.

40. *Till famine cling thee* Until starvation shrivels you up.

40. *If thy speech be sooth* If what you say is true.

Macbeth
> She should have died hereafter;
> There would have been a time for such a word.
> To-morrow, and to-morrow, and to-morrow,
> Creeps in this petty pace from day to day   20
> To the last syllable of recorded time,
> And all our yesterdays have lighted fools
> The way to dusty death. Out, out, brief candle!
> Life's but a walking shadow, a poor player,
> That struts and frets his hour upon the stage,   25
> And then is heard no more; it is a tale
> Told by an idiot, full of sound and fury,
> Signifying nothing.

[Enter a MESSENGER.*]*

> Thou com'st to use thy tongue; thy story quickly.
Messenger
> Gracious my lord,   30
> I should report that which I say I saw,
> But know not how to do't.
Macbeth
>   Well, say, sir.
Messenger
> As I did stand my watch upon the hill,
> I look'd toward Birnam, and anon methought
> The wood began to move.
Macbeth
>   Liar and slave!   35
Messenger
> Let me endure your wrath, if't be not so.
> Within this three mile may you see it coming;
> I say, a moving grove.
Macbeth
>   If thou speak'st false,
> Upon the next tree shalt thou hang alive,
> Till famine cling thee. If thy speech be sooth,   40

41. I don't care if you do the same to me (i.e. bind me alive to a tree).

42–4. *I pull in ... like truth* I find I doubt my own certainty and begin to wonder whether the Devil (speaking in the form of the Third Apparition, the Child Crowned) mislead me by lying, even though seeming to tell the truth.

46. *Arm, arm, and out* He shouts orders to make an attack on the besieging army.

47–8. *If this ... tarry here* i.e. If what this messenger says is true. It won't make any difference whether we try to escape or stay here in the castle.

49. *gin* begin.

50. *th' estate o' th' world* the ordered universe.

51. *the alarum bell* the bell warning the men in the castle that an attack is coming.

51. *wrack* destruction.

52. *harness* armour. Macbeth regains a touch of his old courage and zest for battle.

I care not if thou dost for me as much.
I pull in resolution, and begin
To doubt th' equivocation of the fiend
That lies like truth. 'Fear not, till Birnam wood
Do come to Dunsinane.' And now a wood   45
Comes toward Dunsinane. Arm, arm, and out.
If this which he avouches does appear,
There is nor flying hence nor tarrying here.
I gin to be aweary of the sun,
And wish th' estate o' th' world were now undone.   50
Ring the alarum bell. Blow wind, come wrack;
At least we'll die with harness on our back.

[Exeunt.]

SCENE 6

Malcolm is already showing the calmness and confidence of genuine authority.

1. *leavy* leafy.
2. *show like those you are* i.e. the soldiers are to reveal themselves; the camouflage has served its purpose.

4. *battle* section of the army. Notice that Malcolm now uses the royal *we*. He is growing into his rightful role.

6. *our order* our plan of battle.
7–8. If we can only bring the tyrant's army to battle tonight we will accept defeat if we cannot fight worthily.

10. *clamorous harbingers* noisy heralds, or forerunners.

Scene 6

Dunsinane. Before the castle

[Drum and colours. Enter MALCOLM, SIWARD, MACDUFF *and
their* ARMY *with boughs.]*

Malcolm
Now near enough; your leavy screens throw down,
And show like those you are. You, worthy uncle,
Shall with my cousin, your right noble son,
Lead our first battle; worthy Macduff and we
Shall take upon's what else remains to do,   5
According to our order.
Siward
                                   Fare you well.
Do we but find the tyrant's power to-night,
Let us be beaten, if we cannot fight.
Macduff
Make all our trumpets speak; give them all breath,
Those clamorous harbingers of blood and death.

[Exeunt.]

SCENE 7

Battle is about to begin. Macbeth is still depending on the only saying of the witches that has not yet been proved false *(none of woman born Shall harm Macbeth,* Act 4, Scene 1, lines 79–80).

The battle is presented in the usual manner of the Elizabethan and Jacobean stage. Brief incidents, involving very small numbers of combatants, rapidly follow one after to the other, to produce a sense of excitement and expectation in the audience.

1–2. The image is from a favourite Elizabethan sport, bear-baiting, in which a bear was tied to a stake while dogs attacked it.
2. *course* a round or bout.

6–7. It sounds as though Young Siward already suspects that he is facing Macbeth.

10. *abhorred* hated, loathed.
10–11. *with my sword ... thou speak'st* I'll show you by the way I fight that you lie in suggesting I'm afraid of your name.

12–13. Macbeth still seems invincible. At least he has once more convinced himself that he is.

Scene 7

Another part of the field

[Enter MACBETH.]

Macbeth

They have tied me to a stake; I cannot fly,
But bear-like I must fight the course. What's he
That was not born of woman? Such a one
Am I to fear, or none.

[Enter YOUNG SIWARD.]

Young Siward

What is thy name?

Macbeth

                Thou'lt be afraid to hear it.   5

Young Siward

No; though thou call'st thyself a hotter name
Than any is in hell.

Macbeth

              My name's Macbeth.

Young Siward

The devil himself could not pronounce a title
More hateful to mine ear.

Macbeth

             No, nor more fearful.

Young Siward

Thou liest, abhorred tyrant; with my sword   10
I'll prove the lie thou speak'st.

[Fight, and YOUNG SIWARD slain.]

Macbeth

              Thou wast born of woman.
But swords I smile at, weapons laugh to scorn,
Brandish'd by man that's of a woman born.

16. *still* for ever.
17. *kerns* Irish foot-soldiers, paid to fight, as Macduff says.
18. *staves* shafts of spears
18–20. *either thou, Macbeth ... undeeded* Macduff now will not fight anyone but Macbeth. His overwhelming desire is to take revenge for the fate of his family.
20. *undeeded* without having done any deeds in battle.
20. *There thou shouldst be* That's where you're likely to be.
22. *bruited* announced by noise.

Stage Direction *Exit* Macduff goes off, seeking Macbeth, and the audience is left in suspense.

24. *The castle's gently render'd* 'The castle has been surrendered with remarkably little resistance'.
25. We have already heard, from Macbeth himself, that many of his men have gone over to the other side (Act 5, Scene 3, lines 7–8). The process must have sped up by now.
27. *The day ... yours* i.e. Your victory is now almost won.

28–9. *foes That strike beside us* enemy soldiers who deliberately miss with their sword thrusts.

[Exit. Alarums. Enter MACDUFF.*]*

Macduff
That way the noise is. Tyrant, show thy face.
If thou beest slain and with no stroke of mine,   15
My wife and children's ghosts will haunt me still.
I cannot strike at wretched kerns whose arms
Are hir'd to bear their staves; either thou, Macbeth,
Or else my sword with an unbattered edge
I sheathe again undeeded. There thou shouldst be;   20
By this great clatter, one of greatest note
Seems bruited. Let me find him. Fortune,
And more I beg not.

[Exit. Alarums. Enter MALCOLM *and old* SIWARD.*]*

Siward
This way, my lord. The castle's gently rend'red;
The tyrant's people on both sides do fight;   25
The noble thanes do bravely in the war;
The day almost itself professes yours,
And little is to do.
Malcolm
                        We have met with foes
That strike beside us.
Siward
                        Enter, sir, the castle.

[Exeunt, Alarum.]

SCENE 8

Macbeth's death leaves mixed feelings in most people's minds.

1. *play the Roman fool* When an honourable Roman faced defeat he usually thought it his duty to commit suicide (see Shakespeare's *Julius Caesar*).

2–3. *Whiles I see lives ... upon them* As long as I see enemies who are still alive, mortal wounds are better on their bodies than on mine.

4. *Of all men else* More than any other man.

5–6. *my soul ... already* Are we to take this as a sign of lingering human feelings (remorse, for example) in Macbeth? Does the comment change your attitude to him at this point?

8. *terms* words. *Thou losest labour* You're wasting your efforts.

9–10. You can just as easily make a mark with your sharp sword on the uncuttable air as make me bleed.

11. *vulnerable crests* the helmets of men who can be wounded.

12. *a charmed life* a life protected by a magic spell.

12. *must not* cannot.

13. *Despair thy charm* Give up any faith you might have had in your magical protection.

14. *angel* evil spirit. (Angels could be good or bad.)

14. *still* always.

16. *Untimely* prematurely (i.e. before he was ready to be born naturally).

Scene 8

Another part of the field

[Enter MACBETH.]

Macbeth

Why should I play the Roman fool, and die
On mine own sword? Whiles I see lives, the gashes
Do better upon them.

[Enter MACDUFF.]

Macduff

              Turn, hell-hound, turn.

Macbeth

Of all men else I have avoided thee.
But get thee back; my soul is too much charg'd   5
With blood of thine already.

Macduff

              I have no words –
My voice is in my sword: thou bloodier villain
Than terms can give thee out.

[Fight. Alarum.]

Macbeth

             Thou losest labour.
As easy mayst thou the intrenchant air
With thy keen sword impress as make me bleed.   10
Let fall thy blade on vulnerable crests;
I bear a charmed life, which must not yield
To one of woman born.

Macduff

           Despair thy charm;
And let the angel whom thou still hast serv'd
Tell thee Macduff was from his mother's womb   15
Untimely ripp'd.

18. *cow'd my better part of man* crushed my spirit.

19. *juggling* cheating.

20. 'That trick us by saying things that have two meanings'. This is the point at which Macbeth finally gives up reliance on the witches.

21–2. *That keep the word ... our hope!* i.e. their words turn out to be literally true, but the other possible meaning, which inspired hope, proves false.

24. *the show and gaze o' th' time* a popular public spectacle (as at a fair).

25. *rarer monsters* 'strangest freaks'. Monsters, in this sense, such as calves with two heads, were frequently shown at fairs.

26. Sideshows were advertised by paintings on cloth hung from poles. Macduff goes on to describe the caption written under the picture.

27. *Here* in the tent where the freak is exhibited.

29. *baited with the rabble's curse* irritated by the crowd's curses (Macbeth is again comparing himself with a bear; see Scene 7, lines 1–2).

31. *And thou opposed* And though you are here opposed to me.

32. *Yet I will try the last* I will nevertheless go to the very limit (that is, fight to the death).

32–3. *Before my body ... shield* i.e. I hold my shield in front of my body.

33. *Lay on* fight.

35. Malcolm is referring to men who have not reported from the battle – that is, those who may have been killed or wounded.

36. *go off* be killed.

36. *by these I see* judging by the (number of) men I see around here.

38. *your noble son* Young Siward.

39. *paid a soldier's debt* 'given his life'.

40. he had only just become an adult.

Macbeth

    Accursed be that tongue that tells me so,
    For it hath cow'd my better part of man;
    And be these juggling fiends no more believ'd
    That palter with us in a double sense,   20
    That keep the word of promise to our ear,
    And break it to our hope! I'll not fight with thee.

Macduff

    Then yield thee, coward,
    And live to be the show and gaze o' th' time.
    We'll have thee, as our rarer monsters are,   25
    Painted upon a pole, and underwrit
    'Here may you see the tyrant'.

Macbeth

                    I will not yield,
    To kiss the ground before young Malcolm's feet
    And to be baited with the rabble's curse.
    Though Birnam wood be come to Dunsinane,   30
    And thou oppos'd, being of no woman born,
    Yet I will try the last. Before my body
    I throw my warlike shield. Lay on, Macduff;
    And damn'd be him that first cries 'Hold, enough!'

        [Exeunt, fighting. Alarums]

  [Retreat and flourish. Enter, with drum and colours,
MALCOLM, SIWARD, ROSS, LENNOX, ANGUS, CAITHNESS,
        MENTEITH *and* SOLDIERS.*]*

Malcolm

    I would the friends we miss were safe arriv'd.   35

Siward

    Some must go off; and yet, by these I see,
    So great a day as this is cheaply bought.

Malcolm

    Macduff is missing, and your noble son.

Ross

    Your son, my lord, has paid a soldier's debt:

41–3. *The which no sooner ... died* Immediately he had proved his manhood by his fighting quality in carrying out his duty without shrinking, there and then he died like a man.

46–50. Siward's reaction to his son's death is a tough soldier's attitude, but undoubtedly sincere. It is typical of men dedicated to service and is not unlike Macbeth's own view of the soldier's profession when he was honoured and praised at the beginning of the play.

48. *hairs* a pun on 'heirs' – another example of a serious pun.

50. *his knell is knoll'd* his death-bell has been tolled (that is, all necessary formalities have been carried out).

52. *parted* departed.

52. *paid his score* settled all his debts (by doing his duty as a soldier).

55. *The time* The world in our time.

56. *compass'd with thy kingdom's pearl* surrounded by the jewels of your kingdom (the faithful thanes standing around).

57. i.e. they are all thinking what Macduff is putting into words.

He only liv'd but till he was a man; 40
The which no sooner had his prowess confirm'd
In the unshrinking station where he fought,
But like a man he died.

Siward

Then he is dead?

Ross

Ay, and brought off the field. Your cause of sorrow
Must not be measur'd by his worth, for then 45
It hath no end.

Siward

Had he his hurts before?

Ross

Ay, on the front.

Siward

Why, then. God's soldier be he!
Had I as many sons as I have hairs,
I would not wish them to a fairer death.
And so his knell is knoll'd.

Malcolm

He's worth more sorrow, 50
And that I'll spend for him.

Siward

He's worth no more.
They say he parted well and paid his score;
And so. God be with him! Here comes newer comfort

[Re-enter MACDUFF, *with* MACBETH's *head.]*

Macduff

Hail, King! for so thou art. Behold where stands
Th' usurper's cursed head. The time is free. 55
I see thee compass'd with thy kingdom's pearl
That speak my salutation in their minds·
Whose voices I desire aloud with mine –
Hail, King of Scotland!

All

Hail, King of Scotland! *[Flourish]*

61. 'Before I, the king, settle the debt I owe you, by rewarding you for your services'. The short time he mentions is in fact only a few seconds. He rewards them by making them earls. This action also symbolizes his gratitude to King Edward of England, because the rank of earl was an English one.

64–5. *What's more ... time* Whatever else I have to do, which ought to be begun appropriately in a new regime ...

68. *Producing forth* Finding and arresting.

69. Is Malcolm's summing-up of Macbeth and his wife an accurate description of them?

70–1. *by self ... her life* committed suicide.

72. *by the grace of Grace* The personification of grace is God himself.

73. *in measure, time and place* 'in the right proportion, at the right time, in the right place'. Malcolm will be the restorer of order in Scottish society.

Malcolm
　　We shall not spend a large expense of time　　　　　　60
　　Before we reckon with your several loves,
　　And make us even with you. My Thanes and kinsmen
　　Henceforth be Earls, the first that ever Scotland
　　In such an honour nam'd. What's more to do,
　　Which would be planted newly with the time –　　　　65
　　As calling home our exil'd friends abroad
　　That fled the snares of watchful tyranny;
　　Producing forth the cruel ministers
　　Of this dead butcher, and his fiend-like queen,
　　Who, as 'tis thought, by self and violent hands　　　70
　　Took off her life – this, and what needful else
　　That calls upon us, by the grace of Grace,
　　We will perform in measure, time, and place.
　　So thanks to all at once and to each one,
　　Whom we invite to see us crown'd at Scone.　　　　75

[Flourish. Exeunt.]

211

Theme and character index

The central concerns of the play *Macbeth* are not just reflected in its action: Shakespeare weaves his key ideas into the fabric of the play by repeated references in the language and imagery of characters' dialogue. When writing about the play, you will need to focus on how Shakespeare communicates his ideas through his language choices, so an awareness of these patterns of reference is essential. It is worth thinking about whether these patterns are just repetitions, or whether Shakespeare is showing some development in the ideas.

SOLILOQUIES

As discussed in the Introduction, Shakespeare uses Macbeth's soliloquies to chart the fall and mental decline of his tragic hero. However, Lady Macbeth and Banquo also have soliloquies. Why do you think Shakespeare wanted to give the audience an insight into the inner minds of these characters too?

Macbeth: 1.7 1–28; 2.1 33–64; 3.1 46–70; 5.3 19–28; 5.5 19–28

Lady Macbeth: 1.5 1–30, 38–54

Banquo: 3.1 1–10

CHARACTERS' KEY SCENES

Macbeth is on stage in half of the scenes in the play, which shows how he dominates the action. It is interesting to note how other characters' significant appearances are spread through the play. Consider, for example, how few scenes actually feature the witches, and note Macduff's long absence from the action between Act 2, Scene 4 and Act 4, Scene 3.

Macbeth: 1.3; 1.4; 1.5; 1.7; 2.1; 2.2; 2.3; 3.1; 3.2; 3.4; 4.1; 5.5; 5.7; 5.8

The Witches: 1.1; 1.3; 3.5; 4.1

Lady Macbeth: 1.5; 1.6; 1.7; 2.2; 2.3; 3.1; 3.4; 5.1

Banquo: 1.3; 1.6; 2.1; 2.3; 3.1; 3.3; 3.4 (ghost)

Macduff: 2.3; 2.4; 4.3; 5.4; 5.7; 5.8

Malcolm: 1.2; 1.4; 2.3; 4.3; 5.4; 5.6; 5.7; 5.8

CONTRAST

Macbeth is built on a series of contrasts, such as good and evil, loyalty and betrayal, light and dark. Sometimes those different sides are not quite distinct and become blurred, and Shakespeare shows that judgements are not always easy.

Grace and sin: 1.6 30; 2.2 26–33; 2.3 130–132; 2.4 40–41; 3.1 65–68 and 86–89; 3.4 41 and 45; 3.6 26–29; 4.1 44, 104, 131–132, 136–137; 4.2 80–81; 4.3 23–24, 43, 91–95, 108–111, 144–145, 155–159, 189–192; 5.3 26–27; 5.8 71–73

Heaven and Hell: 1.7 7; 2.3 1–20; 3.1 139–140; 4.3 223–227; 5.1 33

Angels and devils: 2.3 4 and 7; 3.4 59; 3.6 45–49; 4.3 22, 117; 5.7 8–9; 5.8 4

Life and death: 2.2 6–8; 2.3 66–68, 75–76 and 91–96; 3.2 19–26; 3.5 4–5; 4.3 165–166, 170–173; 5.8 39–53

Health and disease: 1.3 23–24; 2.2 45–46; 2.3 48; 3.1 105–106; 3.4 53–56 and 86–87; 4.3 141–159 and 214–215; 5.1 53 and 68; 5.2 27–30; 5.3 39–47 and 50–56

Fair weather and foul: 1.3 12–30 and 38; 2.3 53–54; 4.1 50–56; 4.2 19–22

Light and darkness, day and night: 1.4 50–51; 1.5 50–54 and 59–61; 2.1 1–5 and 49–56; 2.3 53–62; 2.4 1–9; 3.1 26–27,

and 135–136; 3.2 40–56; 3.3 9, 14; 3.4 126–127; 4.1 24,
and 46; 4.3 240

Order and disorder: 1.4 24–27; 3.1 91–101 (the extended
comparison with dogs suggests that men have lost their
humanity and the natural human order has been overturned);
3.2 16–19 and 24–26; 3.4 1, 76, 109–110 and 119–120; 3.6
33–37; 4.1 50–58; 4.2 54–56; 4.3 4–8, 66–69, 78–84 and
97–100; 5.5 50

Desire and performance; intention and action: 1.7 39–41;
2.3 26–28; 3.2 4–5; 4.1 144–153

Appearance and reality: 1.3 42–43, 45–47 and 81–82; 1.4
11–12; 1.5 65–66; 1.7 83; 2.2 12–13, 53–55 and 70–71; 2.3
75–76, 101 and 136–137; 2.4 6–10; 3.1 74–77 and 120–121;
3.2 27–28 and 31–35; 3.4 61, 68 and 107; 5.3 26–28; 5.4
4–7; 5.6 1–2

Clothing and the person wearing it: 1.3 108–109 and
145–147; 2.4 37–38; 5.2 20–22

AMBIGUITY
There is a lot of ambiguity in the play – uncertainty about
language and meaning. This gives Shakespeare the opportunity
to play with alternative meanings of words and phrases so
that they can be interpreted in different ways. Equivocation
veils the truth, while a pun plays on different meanings of
the same word. With dramatic irony, Shakespeare creates
tension through the audience's having greater knowledge and
understanding than the characters do. This is perhaps most
striking in the moments before Macduff discovers Duncan's
body in Act 2, Scene 3.

Equivocation: 1.3 122–126; 2.3 8–11 and 28–34; 4.1 78–79
and 90–92; 5.5 42–46; 5.8 12–22

Punning and word-play: 1.5 17–25; 1.7 1–7; 2.2 55–57; 3.4
15; 5.8 48

Dramatic irony: 1.6 20–24; 2.3 40–62 and 83–86; 3.1 126; 3.4 90–91

OTHER KEY AREAS

Nature: References to nature and the natural order are important in a play where characters, like the witches, or actions, like Macbeth's, are considered 'unnatural' (Act 2, Scene 4, line 10 and Act 5, Scene 1, lines 65–66). 1.3 137; 1.4 28–29 and 32–33; 1.5 15–17 and 40–50; 1.6 1–10; 1.7 46–47 and 54–59; 2.1 7–9; 2.2 14–16 and 39–40; 2.3 57–60; 2.4 10–20 and 27–29; 3.1 29–32, 47–49 and 95–97; 3.4 28, 30, 78–83, 115 and 141; 3.6 8–10; 4.1 96–98; 4.2 8–11; 5.1 65–67

Honour: The idea of honour is an important one. Macbeth starts the play as an honourable and honoured soldier, but ends with a very different reputation. 1.2 44; 1.3 104–109 and 145; 1.4 39–42; 1.6 10 and 17–18; 1.7 32–35; 2.1 25–29; 3.2 33; 3.4 40; 3.6 36; 4.2 64; 4.3 117; 5.3 25; 5.8 62–64

Disturbed sleep: The disturbance of sleep is a key indicator of guilt in the play. 1.3 20–21; 2.1 6–9 and 49–51; 2.2 35–43; 3.2 16–19; 3.4 141; 5.1 (Lady Macbeth's sleepwalking scene)

Manhood: Shakespeare explores the question of what it means to be a man in the world of the play. Military strength and courage feature prominently, but there is also consideration of restraint, courtesy, loyalty and compassion. 1.2 24; 1.3 139–142; 1.7 46–47, 49–51 and 73; 2.3 108–109 and 133; 3.1 90 and 99–101; 3.4 58–60, 73, 99–103 and 107–108; 4.2 75–77; 4.3 220–221 and 235; 5.2 10–11; 5.8 17–18 and 39-43

Womanhood: There are not many women in the play: Lady Macbeth, Lady Macduff, Lady Macbeth's attendant, and the three witches – who are ambiguous. Through these few female roles, Shakespeare explores a number of ideas about womanhood. 1.3 45–47; 1.5 40–41 and 47–48; 1.7 54–55; 3.4 64–66; 4.1 78–79; 4.3 230–231; 5.3 4–7; 5.7 2–3 and 11–13; 5.8 13–16 and 31